SILENT MOUNTAIN

S.E. BROMKE

Silent Mountain

PROLOGUE

Logan Zick was a man of routine.

Just like his father. And his father's father. And every Zick man since the Zick ancestors settled Hogtown, Arizona back in the 1800s.

Normally, he woke with the sun, fed himself lukewarm grits out of a cloudy glass bowl, combed his sparse hairs crossways over the top of his head, dressed, and took to the dock with his gear.

He'd cast for a couple hours and fill his cooler before lunch, which would allow him to craft his plain bologna sandwich and swallow it down with a glass of milk before the daily drive into town.

Logan hated going to town. He hated town. He hated everything about Maplewood—what it had become. What it should never have been.

And yet, he carried on and maintained his family's legacy, or what of it he could—principally, living off the land. However, once Sally passed on, he could no longer run the farm. All that was left on the farm was his fishing.

He was forced to turn it into a living, bartering the daily catch for milk, bread, and a bit of cash to cover gas for his Ford, the electricity bill, or an occasional beer.

But hawking fish at the one market in town didn't always cover life.

Sometimes, he picked up an odd job here or there. He was good with small engines, and his cousin who lived in town would often hire him out on referrals for repairs. He had a good working truck, which was all a man needed to pull a twenty here or there. Deliveries were easy money. Especially when the money came from summer people who couldn't wipe their own ass if their hand was sewn to it. Couldn't wipe their own ass if their life depended on it.

On July fifth, a day which promised to be as normal as any other, Logan Zick hefted his bony body out of bed, its frame creaking arrhythmically under his slight build, and trudged to the kitchen to throw together grits, slurping them down automatically. He then returned to the washroom and combed his hair before stepping out into the shed that leaned against his cabin. He grabbed his tackle box, rod, and grimy cooler before plodding the short distance to the dock.

As Logan made his way down the wooden slats that carried him out onto the lake, his irritation grew. He hadn't slept well. The day before was long, and long days vexed his nerves. He'd been forced to deal with people. Tourists.

That wasn't all.

Friday on the mountain meant even more tourists than usual. Even worse than the day before, he reckoned. Once he'd haul his load into his truck, he'd no doubt have to battle an onslaught of weekend warriors. Then he'd arrive at Big Ed's Market, where he'd be met with an exasperated Big Ed, who didn't mind the influx of customers but who certainly seemed to mind Logan and his fish, despite their agreement.

Logan blew out a sigh and bent down to drop the tackle box and cooler onto the dock before checking his rod and reel, rigging the hook with a lure, and casting deftly into the inky water.

Once the line was taut, Logan eased his thin frame into the sun-bleached canvas chair whose legs, over time, had screwed themselves into the dock like dowels. Then he closed his eyes. Warmth spread across his ruddy face and into the sparse hairs of his head as they lifted with the breeze, lulling him into the slow pull of a nap.

A nibble at the end of the line dragged him back to consciousness, and he jolted forward, muttering to himself as he fumbled to tug the line in. As soon as he started to reel, he felt disappointing weightlessness on the other end.

Lost the damn thing.

He recast, hunkered back down, and cleared his throat. Phlegm rattled his vocal cords awake as he shifted in the sunken cloth seat.

Moments passed and he carefully started to reel, testing for action. On the third rotation, the tip of his rod dipped dramatically toward the water.

Damn it.

He was hung up. Carp hadn't been doing jack shit and the bottom weeds were thicker than a pig's hide.

He hoisted himself up, stretched the pole high, and flicked his wrist. To his surprise, the line gave somewhat and pulled back. He tugged quickly and reeled, but the weight at the other end had him convinced, again, that he was hung up.

The old fisherman moved to the far end of the dock and stretched and flicked. For a second time, the line pulled. Must have snagged a wig of weeds or some such shit. Beads of sweat broke out amongst the whiskers on the back of his neck and he muttered a few curses as he reeled the line, fighting against what was sure to be a clump of flora.

At last, the line gave way, snapping off at the surface of the water and sending Logan staggering backward. There was one thing Logan hated worse than tourists, and that was waste. Losing a hook and a lure to the rocky depths of Hogtown Lake—*his* lake—was a recipe for an emotional outburst. If he'd had an audience, he'd be wailing and whining, cursing and foaming with rage.

Instead, he shook his head bitterly, hocked a booger, and spat it in the general direction of his dearly departed rig. Satisfied enough, he dropped to his tackle box and hitched together a new set in seconds flat.

He recast toward the southeast now, despite the blinding sunrise, hoping to avoid another snag. He expected the familiar rhythm of his rig hitting the water with a quiet *thunk* just as his rear end hit the canvas with a *whoosh*.

But as he sat, he didn't hear or feel the *thunk*.

Instead, his line remained slack in his finger grip, the rig never having sunk to the lake bottom. Logan looked back out to where he'd cast, unaware just how second nature it was for him to cast, catch, cast, catch, cast, catch.

His frustration resumed, and he hocked another booger before shielding his eyes from the sun and straining to see if he'd cast too far. If his lure'd landed on the adjacent shore. It'd be hung up again if that were the case.

But as Logan Zick, old-time fisherman and Hogtown original, gazed across the calm, glossy water, he saw that his lure was gleaming like a star in the dead center of the lake.

Atop an island of some sort.

Couldn't be.

Logan muttered another curse. The sun's glare off the water paired with his position on the dock kept him from a good view. Made no sense that a chunk of earth would disembark from the shore and sail away.

The dark mass *had* to be an animal carcass. Maybe a deer.

Yeah, a deer.

Back when Logan was in grade school, a doe had got caught up in the river out past Zick Ranch Road. His cousins called him over to watch in morbid fascination as the doe struggled for some time. As the boys went back and forth over whether to risk their own lives and free her, one of the Zick moms called them all in for supper. That settled the matter.

When they returned the next day, the doe was dead. They weren't sure if she'd drowned or what. The Zick boys spent the following weeks pelting the carcass with BBs.

Logan moved back down the dock and picked his way through the brambles and over roots closer to the middle of the lake.

The shape grew clearer as he edged up to the water and

narrowed his eyes under the shield of his sun-spotted hand.

It wasn't a bloated doe with matted fur and a wide torso perfect for target practice like the one in his mind's eye.

Dread fell over the old man.

It wasn't a doe at all.

Oh, how he wished it were.

CHAPTER 1

Bo Delaney chewed on a hangnail as she crested Maplewood Boulevard away from the office and toward the
lodge.

It was her second week at the *Mountain Times*, and she
was surprisingly content. Not happy, per se, but content.

Staying at her sister's bed-and-breakfast was the worst
part of moving back home. Perhaps it would have been
better if she'd accepted her parents' offer at the farm. Too
late now.

Then again, half the reason she came back up to the
mountain was to help Mary with housekeeping and cook-
ing. Ever since rebranding last winter, business at Wood
Smoke was booming. And summer on the mountain? The
place was booked till Labor Day. Overbooked, in some
cases. Besides, now that Mary was engaged, she was
becoming increasingly distracted in her business practice.
She needed Bo.

So, after a few hours at the paper, Bo would battle

tourist traffic and head back up the mountain to her evening gig, as she called it.

The job at the paper was fine. Good, even. Helping at the lodge was okay, too. But Bo hated summer on the mountain. She didn't want to hate it. But the tourists gave her no choice. They clogged the main highway in their just-washed-for-the-trip SUVs. They stole the good tables at Darci's, spreading their oversized parties across whole sections of the cozy cafe. And once they left, they were never really gone. The ongoing discovery of cheap beer cans studding the lake shores was proof enough of that.

She turned her radio up and tuned out the throng of caravans, motorcycles, and the noise that a small town wasn't supposed to suffer.

A minivan pulled out of Irma's Antiques and Curios, causing Bo to slam on her breaks and swerve to the shoulder. She laid on the horn and threw up the bird at the aloof idiots before revving her engine and resuming her position at the back of the pack. Bo grabbed for her phone, ready to snap a photo of the minivan's license plate. But a truck had run up behind her. Bo steadied her gaze in her rearview mirror, giving up on the minivan in favor of examining the hot duo of cowboys whose elbows popped out each window.

She finished chewing on her hangnail then let her finger drop. Lifting her chin meaningfully, she locked eyes with the driver, winked, glanced over her shoulder, then cut left and accelerated, passing the line of visitors in order to zoom up the mountain and away from temptation.

Minutes later, Bo pulled into the long treed drive of Wood Smoke. Buzzing from her near collision and the rearview-mirror flirtation that helped cool her heels, she slowed the car and stared out at the property she now called home.

Mary's maples and aspens were lush, and Bo drank in their color as she parked and sat for a moment, running her hand along her dash to test for dust and glancing around her front seat for errant straw wrappers or loose change. Still not quite ready to face the afternoon rush of check-ins, Bo killed the engine and let the warmth of the sun penetrate her windshield and quiet her. She took three deep breaths.

One for a clean car.

One for steady income.

And a very deep one for being home again. Near her family. During the summer. She held the last breath until a cough tickled her throat and forced her to let it all out.

Her phone buzzed from the passenger seat.

Bo unclicked her seat belt and reached for it, swiping to read the new text.

A group text from her sister, Mary, addressed mostly to numbers Bo didn't recognize.

Don't forget to check in by 5 tomorrow night. Party kicks off at 6. See y'all real soon!

Bo cringed. She was not looking forward to attending Wood Smoke's First Annual Sweet Summer Soiree. It sounded cheesy and lame and too fun. Bo didn't really like fun. And since when did Mary start saying "y'all"?

The only number she recognized in the thread was Anna's, her younger sister. She could safely assume Mary's fiancé was also in there. And Anna's boyfriend. She had no clue who else was staying over for the party weekend.

Bo slid her phone into her satchel and crawled from her little car before trudging through raked gravel and up the deck steps into the lodge. She glanced at the cuckoo clock that hung above Mary's key rack and noted the time.

Behind the old wooden desk perched Mary on her stool, carefully scrawling out a line into her log as a trio of college-aged kids laughed and paraded into the great room. Mary glanced up at Bo, rolling her eyes above a half-smile as she kept writing. Bo joined her behind the desk, dropping her satchel to the ground and looking over Mary's shoulder to check the room numbers on the log.

Mary loved tourists. They were her business, after all. But she sympathized with Bo, too. All locals did, really.

"Room number five?" Bo confirmed as she looped the old-fashioned key ring over her thumb and grabbed the brochure packets from the pile on the shelf under the desktop.

Mary nodded before correcting her with the room *name*. "Squirrel. Remember, Bo, we're selling an experience." Then she peered around the corner, watching as the giggling threesome sank into the sofas, propped their feet on the coffee table, and generally acted like children who were away from their parents for the first time.

Accepting the correction without a fight, Bo took over. "What's the name of their party?"

"Robinson."

"Robinson," Bo called from the corner of the desk. "Your room is ready."

They meandered back, dragging mismatched overnight bags along the hardwood. One boy. Two girls. Maybe it was the journalist in her, always hunting for a story—salacious or not—but Bo couldn't help but wonder how this group functioned. One couple and a third wheel? Just friends?

Bo eyed each one as the apparent leader filed up to grab her key.

The two girls were the epitome of millennialism. High-waisted short shorts. Crop tops revealing underboob and feathery rib tattoos. Overdone eyebrows set above long lashes and dewy cheekbones.

The boy, oddly, was a dope. Soft in body and less fashionable, he didn't fit. Tucked away behind the girls, he carried a duffle slung low along his jean shorts.

Bo didn't like them.

The dopey boy discretely scratched his crotch. "So, where's the best fishing 'round these here parts?" He laughed at himself. The girls rolled their eyes. Mary blinked.

"Well, as a matter of fact, you can find a little map and some basic information here in your brochure!" She waved toward Bo's outstretched hand. "And if you have any questions, don't hesitate to ask. Bo and I know the mountain like the backs of our hands."

Bo let out a sigh and forced a smile. "Here ya go," she said as she passed the packet over to the crotch-scratcher.

"This way, everyone!" Mary chirped, cheerful as ever to have another fully booked lodge.

Bo kept her eye on the bizarre party as they made their way through the kitchen and dining room, out the back deck, back in, and up the stairs to their room. They'd be down soon enough to go for an afternoon hike and grab dinner at Jimmy Jake's Steaks or some other local establishment-turned-tourist-trap. After that, they'd wind up at the Brew House, where they'd no doubt find themselves too drunk to drive back. Upon realizing that Uber doesn't exist in Maplewood, they'd attempt to walk back to the lodge, getting lost a few times before one of them sobered up enough to call the lodge and ask for help from the down-home innkeeper herself.

Mary, no doubt, would answer the call, sleepily, in her tatty robe, and give them simple directions before flipping on the porch light and settling into the love seat to ensure her guests made it back.

That's exactly how it would go. Bo learned this quickly in her brief time there. Feeling bad for Mary, she began to join her in the wee hours of the morning. They'd doze together on the love seat. In fact, only a couple days earlier, Bo even offered to go pick up the foolish guests who'd wandered a little too far from the beaten path.

However, Mary had told her no. That it was never wise to offer strangers a ride late at night, as though Bo hadn't considered that. She was only trying to help. And with her hatred of out-of-towners, it was any wonder she'd offered at all. Her love of sleep overpowered her frustration with the idiots.

Once the threesome went up upstairs and into their rooms, Bo grabbed her satchel and did the same, slipping quietly behind the group and down the hall after everyone had disappeared behind pinewood doors. She stalled near the door to see if she could hear her new neighbors and suss out any juicy info on the hodgepodge group.

Female murmurs floated through the pine walls. A laugh came and went.

After plugging in her phone to charge, Bo locked her

room and went back downstairs where she found Mary in the kitchen, prepping a snack.

"Gonna get real busy around here tomorrow," Mary commented as Bo snuck a triangle of watermelon from the serving tray.

"I know. Kurt, Anna, Dutch. Who else?"

Mary nibbled on a rind and answered, "Kurt, yes. Anna and Dutch, yes. And two of their friends. You might remember the guy from when Kurt bought his lot up here. The architect from Mesa. Michael. And his wife, Kara."

Those were the unfamiliar numbers.

Bo knew Mary was excited about the event. It would bring local attention to the lodge in addition to spreading the word to visitors. Wood Smoke had recently become more than a sleepy bed-and-breakfast. With the help of Anna's marketing prowess, Mary had managed to turn it into a retreat and an event locale. It had come to life.

In fact, Mary was hosting the Sweet Summer Soiree for the public, not just the guests. She planned every detail, excited for Wood Smoke to enjoy a little notoriety on the mountain.

Their brothers would be setting up a cider station. Darci's Cafe was catering brats and beer. A local band would perform under the pine trees.

Mary wiped her hands on her stiff apron before whisking the tray up and out to the great room side table, where it would join a lemonade pitcher and a set of mason-jar drinking glasses. The three other rooms upstairs were also booked. But those guests were out and about, taking in the few sights Maplewood had to offer. A lake. A trail. Antique stores. That kind of thing.

The sisters posted up at the reception desk, awaiting the small-but-rowdy bunch to descend from above, grab their snacks, and leave.

Guests didn't typically hang around the lodge. It functioned much like any run-of-the-mill hotel: A place to hang your hat. Dry your boots. Shut your eyes for the night.

"Are your other guests coming to the party?" Bo asked.

Mary thought about it. "I would think so. They're surely invited." She smiled up at the threesome.

Once the young trio had come and gone, Mary clapped her hands together.

"Kurt is getting into town tonight, and he might stay here," she admitted as a blush bloomed across her cheeks.

Bo smiled at her littlest sister. Mary had always been a prude, but Bo loved that about her. She had . . . principles. Everyone could learn a thing or two from Mary. It was a rare event when Mary would forego her morals in favor of . . . whatever she and Kurt had planned for the evening.

"Really?"

Mary locked the register and closed her log, avoiding Bo's gaze. "Well, Kurt offered to help set up tomorrow, and we figured the earlier we start the better. After all, won't it be fun to have a big group of our friends and family? Like a little reunion!"

Bo didn't argue. After all, better the devils you knew than the tourists you loathed.

CHAPTER 2

Brittany sipped up the last of her Diet Coke. Well. *Jack* and Diet Coke.

God *bless* America.

God bless liquid courage. Though Brittany hardly needed liquid courage. She'd laid low for over a day before driving herself the four hours out of Scottsdale, around the canyon, and up the mountain.

She'd only stopped once. At the gas station outside of town. She knew full well her card would place her there, but she also knew her head start would allow her at least one last confrontation. One last attempt. And anyway, he'd probably come to his senses when he realized she was willing to risk it all for him.

Two years before, Brittany hadn't been surprised when Kurt asked for the divorce. She wasn't sad, either. She wasn't sad when the paperwork was finalized. She wasn't sad when she heard that Kurt started his own business. Nor was she sad when she heard his business hit multimillion-dollar status.

Brittany was not sad to learn that Kurt had met someone.

But, in February, she had texted Kurt. Reached out to him. Offered a truce. A peace. A chance to start over and return to her. They could get together somewhere quiet. She pictured their toast. "To new beginnings." She could taste the velvety red wine as though it was coating her gullet right now. Oh, wait. That was the Jack.

Kurt did not only turn her down, he blocked her. Blocked her number. Blocked her on social media. Blocked her from following his company's social media. He blocked her email address. And he blocked the three new email addresses she'd made for the exclusive purpose of explaining things to him. Explaining to him that they were meant to be. All he had to do was reply.

But he never replied.

And Brittany became very sad.

CHAPTER 3

Most cops hated the Fourth of July. Especially Maplewood cops. But Keegan Flanagan wasn't a cop. He was a sheriff with the Apache County Search and Rescue Division. Yet, in Maplewood, all law enforcement officers were on call for the Fourth. In a town so small with a tourist population so booming, that's just how it went.

While he wasn't technically working, he would have to spend his day on edge. At any moment, he could be called to a Drunk and Disorderly or the like.

Keegan pulled on a T-shirt, its sleeves cutting into his biceps. He then grabbed a pair of sweats and tugged them on over his boxer briefs and lastly pocketed his wallet. Once he was dressed and ready, he locked up his one-room cabin.

A few years before, Keegan's father had retired from his executive position with Maplewood Bank and Trust, the only financial business in the area. But retirement didn't suit him. So, he decided to run for city office. Bob Flanagan landed the mayor gig with ease, thanks in part to his contacts and in part to his wife's contacts. Victoria Fiorillo-Flanagan was the top-performing realtor in the region, exclusively selling houses to Valley visitors or Maplewood bigwigs.

Keegan and his three younger brothers, Billy, Danny, and Patrick, grew up in a sprawling estate on the eastern rim of the mountain. With a guest house and a five-car garage, the Flanagans were Maplewood royalty.

But Keegan didn't like that life.

Instead, once he'd graduated from the academy and returned home, he found himself a small plot of land near Maplewood Lake. He camped out there day and night as he and a couple of his buddies built a log cabin from scratch. Keegan had basked in the experience. Sure, as a kid, he was trained to camp and hunt like any other mountain boy, but taking on this project away from his family was formative. Life-changing. It made him a man.

Keegan pulled each leg into a quick stretch, then twisted his torso and swung his arms for a quick warm-up before setting off from his porch toward the lake, where he ran four laps. Four miles a day, every day except for weekends and holidays.

In the summer, the lake was packed at all hours. Even a six a.m. run wasn't early enough to avoid tourists. Keegan didn't mind them; he was happy to move around the old-timers and visiting families, easily keeping his pace as he gazed right over the still, clear water.

Once he'd wrapped up the jog, he walked the half-mile back to his cabin, where he grabbed a quick shower and shave. He changed into one of his work polos and a pair of jeans before lacing up his boots and sliding his wallet into the familiar space of his back pocket.

Crossing to his kitchen cabinet, he opened it only to remember that he was out of coffee. He considered his options: Darci's for a sit-down sip at the bar, where he'd no doubt field questions from the line-up of local regulars. How was the department? How was Bob? Victoria? His brothers?

No thanks.

There was the drive-through joint: JavaTime. Keegan didn't care for designer coffee.

Big Ed's would probably be packed with summer folks and locals alike. But he might as well grocery shop now, before it got any worse.

He grabbed his keys and locked up, descending his porch steps and crossing to his carport where his truck sat waiting. Pulling himself in, he started the engine and took off toward the market.

Once he arrived, his predictions proved accurate. The parking lot teemed with vehicles of all makes and models. Even the neighboring dirt lot was filling up. Keegan waited as a rusty pick-up reversed out of one of the far spots in the lot, leaving him to pull in and shut off the ignition.

AC blasted the smell of freshly baked breads as he strode through the automatic door. It took some deft weaving through the splash of customers as he grabbed a basket and began to fill it with essentials. Bread, fruits, veggies, a few protein bars, and a couple of frozen entrées took him to the far side of the store. Once he moved to the dairy section, a barricade of three college-aged kids blocked his path. Two girls and one guy. Keegan stepped up against the beer case, waving a hand dramatically to let them pass.

As they neared, the girls trained their eyes on him. The tallest, a blonde with long legs made longer by short shorts and a barely-there tank top, pointed to him.

"Well, hello, Mountain Man," she purred to her friend, keeping her eyes on Keegan. They fell into wild giggles. The poor schmuck behind them pretended to study a can of soup. Keegan smirked before averting his gaze beyond them to a more familiar face.

Bo Delaney.

"It's like the mountain is a zoo, and we're the animals," she said once the three tourists moved on to the liquor aisle. Keegan's eyes passed over Bo, taking in her dark hair, piercing eyes, and pale skin. She was dressed in worn jeans and a plain white T-shirt. It was as though she had stepped out of high school and into adulthood without a hitch. She was grown-up and gorgeous.

Keegan swallowed hard. He hadn't seen her in a while. He wondered if she was still into jerks like his brother. He laughed and nodded his head in agreement. "Back for vacation, *Roberta*?"

"Don't call me that, Keegan." She glared before allowing a smile to spread across her lips. "Not a visit this time." She glanced over her shoulder as another throng of people squeezed by. The two moved closer to the refrigerated case. And each other.

"What does that mean?"

"I'm living here, again. Got a job with the paper. Reporter gig. Right now, just fluff pieces, but we're hoping to broaden my section. Got any juicy gossip for me?" She teased as she drew a finger to her mouth and nibbled on the nail. High school memories flashed through his head. Bo peeking out from the far side of Billy while they sat three across in a darkened movie theater. Bo throwing a curious glance to Keegan in Spanish class. Bo. Bo. Bo.

Keegan was aloof in high school. But he saw Bo. Always had. Still did, sometimes.

He played along, winking and lowering his voice. "Word has it the fireworks display may be delayed by half an hour. But you didn't hear that from me."

She let out a hearty laugh, her face softening and body relaxing. Keegan moved his eyes back to hers. "Well, Bo, in all seriousness, welcome back to the mountain. I, for one, am glad you're here."

Bo waited to reply, keeping her gaze level to match his. "Thanks, Keegan. Me, too." A broad smile now brightened her face and she let her hand slip into her jeans pocket.

After she left without little more than a wave, Keegan finished his shopping trip, returning to his lonely cabin near the lake. Once he'd put away his groceries, he grabbed his phone off his bed and began to put together a text to his two pals. He may be on call, but that didn't mean he couldn't at least go somewhere, for once. Do something fun, for once.

The responses were quick. His cousin, Irving, was taking the kids to the parade. Jake was out of town. Before tossing the phone back to the bed, a realization dawned on him.

Wood Smoke was having some sort of party. He'd seen fliers everywhere. Even one of the guys from the department was talking about it. The force had been apprised of all the local events in order to set up DUI stops.

But no, he couldn't go. Bo's little sister owned Wood Smoke. Bo might be there. That'd be weird. Instead, Keegan decided he'd stroll downtown for the fireworks, keep an eye on the activity, and—with any luck—head back home for a good night's sleep before what was sure to be a crazy day tomorrow.

CHAPTER 4

Bo swung into the kitchen of Wood Smoke, her news for her sister urgent. "You'll never guess who I saw at Big Ed's."

Mary swiveled around, her hands elbow deep in yellow rubber gloves as she sidestepped Kurt who dutifully unloaded the dishwasher.

"Throw me that roll of paper towels, Bo," Mary directed. Bo did as she was told and followed her sister to the back deck to help clean windows. Kurt rustled behind them, reloading the dishwasher. "Who?" Mary asked as they got to work spraying and wiping.

"Keegan Flanagan," Bo deadpanned, pausing to catch Mary's reaction.

She didn't even flinch. "I definitely could have guessed that. I see him all the time." The push and pull of wadded-up paper towels squeaked across an especially grimy square inch of pane. Bo's shoulders fell and she frowned.

"Aren't you interested in our interaction?"

Mary stopped and her hand dropped from the pane.

"I'd assume that you said hello and went your separate ways."

Bo rolled her eyes. "Did you forget? I dated Keegan's brother in high school."

"Yeah, Bo. How could I forget? You and Anna and the Flanagan boys. It was awful. You were so wild together. They were so . . . mean. Bullies, really."

Bo finished her area and surveyed the deck. "Well, I guess I just . . . never mind. It was just interesting seeing him. He's . . . he's so different than his brothers."

"I was too young to know. We weren't even in high school at the same time."

Bo realized this, but she would have loved to flesh it out with Mary. Talk through her unresolved feelings from high school. No one knew the full story. No one knew that Bo only dated Billy to get closer to Keegan. Bo crushed hard on the oldest Flanagan brother. Too hard. So hard, in fact, that Keegan was one of the reasons Bo struggled to return to Maplewood. She didn't want to lose face after so many years of so little success.

Kurt wandered out through the door, inspecting the glass. "Looks great. What's next?"

Mary told Kurt to start setting up tables, and Bo offered to join. He gave Mary a playful spank, at which Bo felt supremely embarrassed. But Mary laughed it off and went back inside to tackle the next task. They had a ton to do before the party, and the caterers and band would be setting up in just hours.

"So how do you like being back on the mountain, Bo?" Kurt's attempt at small talk was sweet enough, and Bo went along. She enjoyed the chance to get to know Mary's fiancé. It felt important. After some back-and-forth about Bo's job at the paper, she shifted attention to him.

"So, Kurt, when will you cut the cord with Phoenix and move here full-time? Have you sold your condo?"

With a folding table tucked under one arm and a stack of chairs dangling from the other, he answered her naturally. "I'll never totally cut the cord. I'm staying on as co-president of the company, and I'll probably just keep the condo for overnight business trips. But my cabin up here is underway. I'll be working out of an in-home office come August."

Bo's mind wandered to Kurt's past. In many ways, he didn't seem like Mary's type. She was a true small-town, mountain girl. She shunned the big city in favor of a quiet life.

Then again, life at the lodge had been anything but quiet all summer. Maybe Mary would move to Kurt's cabin sooner than later. Of course, Mary didn't believe in shacking up. She was entirely traditional. Pure, even. Which was another reason Bo didn't understand her interest in Kurt.

He was divorced.

———

The cuckoo clock struck five, and Bo stood at the front door, admiring their hard work. The lodge was cleaner than it had ever been. Scrubbed, vacuumed, and shined to a polish. Americana splashed across the front door, the reception desk, the great room side table, and on out to the backyard, where the band was warming up to the sizzle of the grill and hum of a margarita machine. The event didn't start until six, but that evening's guests were due to check in at any moment.

Mary descended the staircase, clad in a red sundress. Navy wedges pinched her little feet. She was beaming, and her excitement was catching. Bo allowed herself a grin. "You look great, Mare. I'm so proud of you."

Mary wrapped her older sister in a tight squeeze before pushing back. "Thanks, Bo."

Bo started to ask if she ought to change into something nicer but was cut off by the sight of Kurt on the landing above them. Mary whipped around, following Bo's gaze.

"Oh my *gosh*, Kurt Cutler. You look gorgeous," Mary gushed. And he did. A styled crew cut framed his broad forehead. Sun-kissed skin glowed from beneath a navy-blue polo and light khakis. Loafered feet grounded him at the base of the steps as Mary ran off into his arms.

Bo glanced away as they kissed, waiting for any sort of distraction to remove her from the weirdness of seeing her little sister make out with a guy like Kurt.

As if on cue, the front door popped open. Anna's red hair fell into the seam as she peeked her nose through the crack. "Knock, knock! Party's here!" She squealed as she pushed the door the rest of the way open, her star-studded jeans flashing beneath a starched white halter. "U. S. A!" She chanted as three others filed in behind her.

Months ago, Bo had met Dutch, Anna's boyfriend, and he came right up to her, wrapping a muscled arm around her neck before stepping back to allow Anna to make introductions.

"Okay, you guys remember Michael Erinhard, right?" Anna glanced around the group that had formed in front of the reception desk. The unfamiliar man offered a cocky half-smile and waved his hand. His gaze paused on Bo, and they locked eyes for a second. What was it with attractive men today? She came to Maplewood to escape temptation, not drown in it.

Michael nodded and turned his head back to a chestnut-haired pip of a woman. "This is my wife, Kara. Kara, this is Mary and Kurt, if memory serves?" They nodded and offered their hands to the mousy woman. "And this is Anna's other sister . . ."

"I'm Bo." She stepped forward, glancing at Michael then back to Kara before taking her slight hand in a brief shake. "Welcome to Maplewood!" Bo tried her hardest to put on a cheerful, patriotic face. She'd kept reminding herself that tonight was important to Mary. It was a chance to spend time with her sisters, too. She could overlook the obnoxious flatlanders who came to the mountain to get drunk. Bo could keep the peace. At least for one night.

"Oh, no need to welcome me. We have a second home here," Kara sneered. Michael let out a chuckle before redirecting the conversation.

"Yep, but we're excited to rough it a little." Michael winked at Mary.

Bo glared at him and lifted her chin before trilling out room numbers and commanding everyone to unload and meet up on the back deck for happy hour.

Michael Erinhard wasn't going to ruin Mary's special night. Not on Bo's watch.

Bo had showered and blown her hair out, dressing simply in denim shorts, a white T-shirt, and Birkenstocks. Whereas before she felt underdressed, now she didn't care. She was proud to look the part of casual local. Nothing to get excited about. Just another day in paradise. Mountain time. All that.

As the latest guests carried their overnight bags upstairs, Mary fluttered to the guest log and made a couple notes.

"Mary, just tell me where to go," Kurt said, his hands stuffed into his khaki pockets.

The hostess spun in a circle before pressing a finger to her mouth. "For now, why don't you wait for Anna and everyone to come back down, then bring them outside. Thanks, Babe."

He gave her a peck before she scurried off, leaving him alone with Bo yet again.

"So, did you invite any friends for the party?" Bo asked, knowing full well that Kurt was something of a loner. Maybe that was why his ex had divorced him, in fact. He'd had few friends apart from his coworkers, according to Mary.

"Actually, yes. Mary was generous enough to invite the guys from work." Kurt peered down at Bo, a shadow crossing his face.

She lifted an eyebrow in question.

He went on, "In fact, you guys might hit it off. You're sort of quirky. They're computer nerds. I'll be sure to personally introduce you." He winked at her.

Bo gagged. No thanks.

She was responsible for overseeing the trash cans. As soon as beer bottles started poking their necks above the rim, Bo was to alert Kurt and help him change out the bags.

This was a fine task for Bo, who wanted an excuse to avoid socializing. She was much more content to people watch.

And people watch she did. Mary's advertising had paid off. Everyone in Maplewood seemed to show up.

Mayor Flanagan and his bitchy wife.

Bo's boss, Paul, and his brother, Stewart.

She wondered if any of the Flanagan boys would make an appearance. Hopefully not Billy. But it might be nice to see Keegan again.

The older couple who were Wood Smoke guests strolled past her, sipping their margaritas and commenting on the cooler weather.

It was eighty degrees out. Humid, too. They must be Phoenix people.

Bo looked around to see if she could spot the obnoxious college trio.

She couldn't.

CHAPTER 5

After a second stop at Big Ed's to grab a six pack, Keegan made his way down the boulevard and to the town square, where he planned to set up a chair, kick back, and relax. Relish the alone time and take in the sights.

As he popped open his canvas chair and cracked a brew, a voice came from next to him.

"Flanagan, is that *you?*"

Keegan turned his head, squinting in the darkness. "Alan? Alan Delaney?"

Keegan and Alan were good friends in high school, but they'd only seen each other in passing around town. What were the odds he'd run into brother and sister in the same day?

After shooting the breeze, Alan explained he was there watching the show with his family, but he had to leave early, because he and his brother were catering a party at his sister's lodge. Keegan played dumb.

"You should come! My sisters will be there. I'm sure they'd get a kick out of seeing you," Alan said.

Should he admit he'd already seen one sister that morning? Probably. "Yeah, well. I saw Bo at the market today. She looks great." It slipped from his lips. But Alan either ignored the compliment or didn't care.

"Yeah, man, you'll have fun. It'll be like old times." It wouldn't be like old times. Old times would include Keegan's asshole brothers who'd long left Maplewood.

Rockets of color splayed across the sky. There was no question, really. He'd always wanted someone with whom to share moments like this. Moments that maybe weren't important, but moments that made a man feel singularly and utterly alone.

Half an hour later, he was pulling in to Wood Smoke behind Alan Delaney. His stomach twisted into knots as he unfolded from his truck to follow Alan around back to where the music and laughter floated from.

Keegan had a crush on Bo ever since his brother brought her on a camping trip back in high school. At the time, she seemed like the whole package. Gorgeous, smart, tough. Why she dated Billy was a mystery to him.

Bo herself was also a mystery to him.

They turned the corner and Alan shouted over to Robbie as he waved his hand wildly. Keegan lifted his hand to Robbie, scanning the crowd as he did. The place was packed. Every seat taken. People milling about in the woods, too. Several more bobbed along as the band played a Willie Nelson number.

At the far side of the clearing, Keegan eyed his own two parents, sipping on margaritas and chatting up a few other familiar faces. He hoped to avoid them entirely.

Robbie strode from his station behind a little wooden bar. "Keegan freakin' Flanagan, how you been, man?"

They shook hands, and Keegan slapped him on the back. "Good, dude, real good. Just followed this asshole to see what you got goin' on tonight." Keegan's drawl came on thick when he was around friends. Despite his nerves at running into Bo, he felt at home out in the woods with a bonfire throwing sparks and country twang echoing from a guitar nearby.

"Cider and margaritas." Alan pointed back to where Robbie had jogged from. "Brewskis and brats." He pointed to a woman standing next to a hot dog stand. "And everything else." He waved a hand toward the back doors of the lodge.

Robbie whipped around. "Anna! Bo! Look who it is!" he shouted through the noisy night. Keegan tugged at the collar of his shirt and followed Robbie's voice to a smattering of chairs near the deck. There, sipping a longneck, was Bo. Her dark hair lifted in the breeze as she stood and muttered something to Anna.

Doubt swelled in him. He shouldn't have come.

Two of his brothers had made their marks on Anna and Bo, but Danny had been especially cruel to Anna.

Keegan didn't blame any of the Delaneys if they never wanted anything to do with a Flanagan ever again. For some reason, though, he was still on good terms with the lot of 'em. He shoved his hands into his pockets as Bo walked up.

"Anna's still pissed at your entire family, in case Alan and Robbie were too clueless to realize."

Keegan glanced at the guys' faces and they shrugged before starting in on a separate conversation about the bar.

Keegan took a step closer to Bo. "I wouldn't blame her. Danny was a Grade A prick back then. Still is, probably, who the hell knows?" He let out a laugh.

Bo slid her eyes down the length of his body and then back up. "Why'd you come?"

"Celebrating the Fourth, of course." He nodded at her empty bottle. "Drink?"

Bo silently agreed, following Keegan to grab a beer and leaving her brothers to return to their station. She accepted a cool, sweaty bottle and tossed her previous one in a nearby trash can.

They stood near the bonfire, quietly working their drinks and listening to the music. He took in the lodge and the scenery. It was a great set up. He said as much.

"Yeah, Mary's got a lot to be proud of."

Keegan cleared his throat. "I didn't have anything goin' on. Saw Alan at the town square and decided to take him up on an offer to come say hello. Hope that's okay," he finished.

She licked her lips and looked up at him. "I'm glad you came, Keegan." He pressed his mouth into a smile and took a swig of his beer. They glanced away from each other before she went on. "Say, this thing wraps up in an hour or so. Some of us are gonna ditch the summer scene and head to Last Chance after. You wanna come?"

He nodded in agreement before Bo excused herself to help Mary. It gave Keegan the opportunity to observe.

Most of the faces glowing above the bonfire and in front of the band were unfamiliar. Young. College kids. Twenty-somethings. One or two older couples peppered the crowd.

He hadn't seen his dad or mom again, nor the folks they'd been chatting with.

Forty-five minutes later, cleanup began. Guests headed their separate ways. One couple went into the lodge, calling it a night. A group of what had to be teenagers scattered into the woods, cackling and wobbling between the pines.

Amongst the outflux, two familiar men slunk down in deck chairs, quietly sipping at their beers and glancing back into the lodge on occasion.

Keegan stepped up to the deck. They stood, and one held out a hand. "Sheriff, isn't it?" the cowboy-type asked.

"That's right. Flanagan. Keegan Flanagan. You're . . . Anna's friend?" He asked, embarrassed in case the guy knew his brother's history with Anna.

"That's right. Boyfriend, I suppose. Dutch McCree. We met back in June, I think. Last time Anna and I were around."

Keegan shook Dutch's hand before opening his grip to the other man. "Yes, and you're Mary's fiancé? The Phoenix tech guy?"

"Kurt Cutler. Good to see you again, Keegan." Kurt was smoother than Dutch. Unnaturally so. He acted, almost, like a movie star or something. A famous person. It unnerved Keegan.

Kurt gestured inside. "I guess the girls are taking us to a local watering hole. Maplewood's best kept secret?"

Keegan smiled and nodded in time for the back door to open. It was Bo.

"Alright, guys, let's do it. You coming, Flanagan?" An eyebrow lifted and Keegan made a split decision to follow Dutch and Kurt through the door, stopping briefly to grab Bo's elbow.

"I'm on call," he murmured as the others joined Mary and another couple at the front door.

Bo glanced up. "So?"

"I can't drink any more. Maybe I should drive separately?"

Bo shrugged. "I'll ride with you. We can leave whenever."

A smile formed on his mouth and he followed her to the front, where he met two other new people. Michael and Kara. Dutch's friends from the Valley.

Michael was shorter than the other men, but fit and sharply dressed. Perhaps a little metro, even. Kara was nice-enough looking. Flat brown hair outlined her jaw in a sharp angle. An expensive haircut that didn't quite achieve the desired effect. Her petite build matched Mary's, but the women seemed worlds apart.

Now that they were coupled, talk of carpooling came up. Bo announced she and Keegan would go alone. Anna and Dutch would ride with Mary and Kurt. Michael and Kara would take their own ride. Kara had already begun to complain about being tired, apparently.

Not fifteen minutes later, their little caravan pulled into the dusty lot outside Last Chance. Keegan hadn't been to the joint in a few months, probably. Last time was with Billy and his dad during a brief visit. Keegan wasn't much of a drinker, but he did enjoy two-stepping. Too bad he rarely had a date to join him. Tonight, however, his luck could change.

They clumped together outside before filing into the dimly lit log cabin that was the Last Chance Saloon. As he'd expected, the place was packed. All the locals seemed to congregate there rather than deal with irritating, drunk tourists who, no doubt, wandered their way into every other drinking hole on the mountain.

It was fine, though. Keegan didn't mind, if it meant he could be close to Bo.

Their party squeezed through the throbbing throng of drinkers and dancers and up to the bar. After drink orders, the group squeezed around two free bar stools at the far end, near the restrooms. Keegan posted up behind Bo. Kurt grabbed Mary's hand and dragged her to the dance floor. Shortly after, Anna excused herself to go to the ladies' room with Kara, while Dutch and Michael made small talk over their drinks.

"Is there a deck or something here?" Michael called over to Keegan. "I need some air already, man." He squinted through the dark room, and Keegan nodded and pointed toward an open door to the left of the dance floor. He and Dutch turned to head out, but Dutch threw a glance back as if to see if Keegan was joining them.

What the hell? Never hurt to make new friends. Bo waved him away and turned her attention to grab the bartender.

Sweaty, Wrangler-clad bodies parted as the three men crossed the bar to the deck. En route, Keegan recognized Paul Zick, his dad's best friend. He'd be darned if fate was pushing him into a holiday reunion. His neck began to itch. He really had no intention of chatting up his parents or their cronies. But he couldn't leave now. He was there with Bo. He had to get back to her. Shoot. Bo probably worked with Paul. If she really was writing for the *Times.* Maybe she'd want to bail, too?

Momentum pushed Keegan ahead and out onto the deck, which was equally crowded.

"Shit, forgot my drink," Dutch called over the heads of an older couple who were sharing a cigarette at the railing. Keegan and Michael nodded and moved to the far end of the deck where there was space.

"This place is great," Michael said once they'd settled in the crook of the railing. "It's so . . . real, ya know?"

Keegan pinched his eyebrows at the comment but agreed. It was a nice spot, especially when it wasn't so packed.

He studied the man for a moment. "So, Michael, what do you do in Phoenix?"

"I'm an architect in Mesa. I designed The Cabins project, actually," he answered, his eyes on the gravel lot as a woman parked her car and nearly fell out.

"So that's how you know Dutch, I guess? And Kurt, for that matter? Don't they own lots there?" Keegan wasn't dumb. He'd pieced things together easily on the drive over, with no help from Bo's vague commentary about the delicate relationships between her sisters and the guys.

Michael ignored his question, his eyes narrowing on the young blonde as she teetered in ridiculously inappropriate heels through the gravel and to the door. Keegan kept his eyes on Michael, following his gaze.

Michael swallowed the last of his drink and set it on the ledge. "Now that's a hot piece of ass, right there." He looked up to Keegan, apparently awaiting an equally assholey comment.

Instead, Keegan's brow wrinkled. Before he had the chance to rebuke Michael's observation, Dutch rejoined them with three beers instead of one. "Here ya go, Mike. Keegan." He held out the glass bottles, but Keegan shook his head.

"I appreciate it, man, but I'm done for the night. Thanks. I'll cover your next round, though," Keegan offered, his voice lifting as a breeze swept over the deck, cooling him considerably. He hadn't realized he'd begun to sweat despite the brisk evening air.

Dutch started a discussion on NFL preseason, which Keegan was happy to contribute to. But soon enough, Michael, whose eyes had been trained on the door for some time, excused himself to go back in. Dutch, now edging on drunk, either didn't notice or didn't care and carried on with his lecture about how the Eagles letting Nick Foles go was the stupidest shit in football history. Keegan happened to agree, but his mind had wandered back to Bo.

"I'm gonna head back in," he declared. Dutch, amenable as ever, followed him like a puppy back through the deck as cigarette smoke clouded their trek.

Just before they stepped inside, Keegan threw a glance over his shoulder, past the smoking deck and toward the front door of the bar.

Leaning up against the wall, facing away, was the

blonde in heels. She was talking to a man. Someone close to her height. Not much taller.

Dutch pushed up against Keegan as if to force him inside, but Keegan grabbed the door frame and pressed back out, craning his neck to see who she was talking to.

It was Michael.

CHAPTER 6

Two men.

Two men and she had been in town for two minutes.

The first was a hot shorty. Brittany liked him. But she was too sober. And the night was too young.

The second was a redneck asshole. She didn't like him. And no amount of vodka would change that.

Brittany squinted through the dim light for Kurt. If he saw those two men hit on her, he'd be so jealous. Maybe the new whore he was with would be jealous, too. She probably knew the men. Lusted over them, even. Until Big-City Kurt came along to rescue her from her no-tell-motel-in-the-pines.

Brittany looked for Mary. Little Mary Delaney, who didn't exist online. Whose whorish older sister worked for Kurt and probably slept with him and every guy in Phoenix. Finding out about Mary was only possible through Anna's wide-open social media presence. Open for the world. For every man, woman, and lumberjack to access her and, therefore, her family.

Finding them at the bar had been the hardest part. Brittany had battled the clogged artery that acted as Maplewood's one-and-only roadway in order to make it to the Wood Smoke Lodge. But she'd missed the party.

An older couple was there, sipping hot cocoa on the leather (probably *faux* leather) sofa. They were stupid and kind enough to explain that the others had gone for a nightcap at some hole-in-the-wall joint up the way.

A quick Google search provided exactly one option: The Last Chance Saloon.

It was so fitting. This was Kurt's last chance.

She wondered how he'd react when he first saw her. Brittany wasn't too dumb to realize he might be shocked. He might get physical. Grab her wrists. Hold her against the bar. Force himself to refrain from nuzzling her neck in front of hicks of all shapes and sizes.

She didn't spot either Kurt or Mary. So, she figured she'd beeline for the bar. But first, another little pre-party drink. She pulled a mini bottle of vodka from her purse and downed it fast. Just in time for a local dandy to join her in the middle of the crowded high tops.

"Well, hello stranger."

Brittany swiveled as well as she could.

A third man.

He caught her before she landed on a tableful of half-empty Coors Light.

She twisted in his arms, and before she knew it, he playfully pinned her against the jukebox. She swallowed. Her throat dry and eyes bleary as his face came into focus.

Older, but it was hard to tell how old. Could be forty. Could be sixty. White hair. Silver. Sexy. Tanned skin under the glowing lamp that swung above them. His button-down shirt tucked cleanly into tight, dark denim pants. Boots pointed out from the bottom of long legs.

Brittany looked beyond him for help.

None came.

"You're not from around here, are ya, sweetie?"

White teeth glowed from his mouth and Brittany felt a wave of nausea move up to her throat.

"'Scuse me," she answered, pushing around him in some miracle. He caught her wrist. They locked eyes.

He was hot. For an old guy. She paused and changed tactics, batting her eyelashes and stepping closer. "Maybe you can help me," she purred.

"Oh, I bet I could."

"I'm looking for someone who lives here."

He flashed a smile and nodded. "I happen to know everyone here. Born and bred. I can help you, alright."

"Oh yeah? What do you do up here in the mountains? Chop wood and plow snow?"

He chuckled. "Something like that."

A second man came up behind him, nudging the silver fox that it was time to go. The second man, also tall, also older, glared at Brittany. "Do you need a ride home tonight, ma'am?"

She tucked her hand back into her purse and fingered the last mini bottle of vodka stowed within. "No," she answered, shaking her head.

"Well, if you do," the second man inserted himself between her and the silver fox, "you can call us." He put out a hand for her to shake before elbowing Silver Fox aside. "Paul Zick. Good to meet you. I work for the paper.

This knucklehead here is Bob Durbin. Town Mayor." They both flashed a smile before Paul added, "Give us a call if you need anything while you're in town. And don't mind the mayor. He's only being friendly." He pressed a card into her hand.

Brittany nodded and they ushered themselves away and out the door. She downed her last bottle and staggered to the bar.

CHAPTER 7

Bo watched and listened with removed interest as Kara pouted and whined. She was *tired*. She was worried she'd have a *hangover*. She felt a little *nauseous*. She had the beginnings of a *headache*.

So, Bo did the only logical thing and recommended she head back to the lodge. Get a good night's sleep. All that.

Bo glanced around the dark bar, desperately searching for Keegan, Dutch, or Michael. She caught a glimpse of Michael, his head ducked down as he struggled through the crowded tables and out the gaping front door. Bo thought she caught a glimpse of a woman's silhouette, but Michael pulled the bar door closed behind him before she could tell.

Bo looked back to Kara, whose head was in her hands on the table. "Let's go get Michael and get you home. How does that sound?" she suggested.

Kara's head snapped back. "Yes, please, God." She rubbed at her temples and sipped from the Jack and Coke that sat sweating on a paper coaster in front of her. Its condensation dripped down, soaking the circle through to the waxed bar top.

"Hey, girls."

Bo spun around, her face warming to Keegan's familiar drawl. He looked exceptionally hot that night. Hotter than he had in high school when he was a brooding senior and she a wild junior. Hotter than he had when she joined his brother and him on a camping trip and Keegan secretly offered her what *he* thought was her first sip of beer.

Age had served him well.

Keegan's tall stature was offset by a muscular build. Cuffed sleeves revealed thick veins running into the backs of his hands as they flexed on the bar top next to her. His gold-flecked green eyes glowed in the shadows of the Last Chance.

Bo lifted an eyebrow. "Hey." She felt the room shrinking in around them. Dutch wandered off to find Anna. Kara had returned her head to her hands, leaning her bosom on the bar and whining quietly to herself.

If there ever was a better moment, this was it. Bo stood and pressed her body against Keegan's.

"I'm leaving." With surprising force, Kara kicked the barstool out from behind her and into a table full of people. Unsteady on her feet, she charged off, squeezing sloppily through a group of cowboys before holding up a middle finger at no one in particular.

Keegan met Bo's eyes and she shook her head, partially dumbfounded, partially pissed. Keegan pushed off the bar, following Kara to where she had become jammed at the jukebox, shouting obscenities to the innocent folks who were fumbling their quarters into the coin slot despite the live band playing across the bar.

Bo grabbed her satchel from the barstool and followed. Keegan reached for Kara's arm.

"Ma'am," Keegan called over the roar of the room. "You can't leave unless someone is driving you."

Kara twisted her arm from Keegan's. "Screw you, *sheriff*," she spat, quelling a gag as she said it. "Find my husband or else I'm driving myself home to *Mesa*."

Keegan gave Bo a look and then glanced about the room. He gave up and asked Bo to help him walk her out to the parking lot.

The three of them pushed through rhinestone-studded locals, tripping here and there over a pointy boot before spilling through the front door and out onto the stunted pavement that gave way to gravel.

Bo stepped farther out, searching the lot for any signs of Michael. But no one was out there.

Sloppily, Kara began to scream. "Michael! You son-of-a-bitch! MICHAEL!"

Keegan took her shoulders in his hands and gave her a gentle shake. "Kara, Kara. Calm down, we'll find him."

Bo looked up at him, uncertain he'd make any headway. "Maybe we should just drive her back?"

Keegan shook his head. "We gotta find him. I'll stay with her, keep her calm. You go back inside and look around." Bo glanced toward the door. Kara let out another ear-piercing scream. Keegan gave Bo a pleading look.

"Kara, shut the hell up," Bo hissed. "Do you have your car keys or does Michael?"

"I don't *know*, you *bitch*, I just rode here with the bastard," she cried, her body heaving into sobs.

Bo rolled her eyes. "Keegan, drive her back to the lodge. The spare is under the boulder by the deck in the back. I'll go in and get Michael and bring him as soon as I find him, okay?"

Keegan nodded and wrapped an arm around Kara. A pang shot through Bo.

She missed her chance.

And it was all thanks to Phoenix trash.

As she pressed back into the hot bar and moved in and out of cramped tables and crowded patrons, she eyed him at the bar, throwing back a shot glass of amber liquid.

But as soon as she reached him, he vanished again, leaving his warm seat empty. Bo propped her satchel on the stool and flagged the bartender to grab her check. She hated having to make the drive of shame the next morning to pay a forgotten tab.

The bald barkeep held up a finger, asking her to wait, and Bo moved the satchel onto her shoulder and settled onto the bar stool as she did. It's not like Michael was going anywhere. She could take care of her business first. Kara would benefit from the sobering-up time, anyway.

Bo shifted on the stool in time for a tall, thin, unfamiliar blonde woman to sidle up next to her. Her makeup was heavy. Her hair sprayed to within an inch of its life. Bo followed the woman's body down to her feet, which were laced painfully into stilettos.

A wayward visitor? Lost her flock of Valley friends?

The blonde smiled crookedly at Bo. "Mountain men sure are aggressive."

Bo smirked in response and raised her eyebrows at the woman.

"One of them just accosted me at the door. Asking for my number and trying to kiss me. What a total rapist, right?" Her smile gave way to a jeer.

Bo looked again for the barkeep, trying to ignore the woman. Two nuts in one night? What were the chances?

"Anyway, I'm married," she slurred, fingering a ring on her left hand.

Bo broke, taking the bait. "You from around here?"

"No," she answered, lifting her purse onto the bar and leaning against it. "But my husband has a place here." She smacked her lips together and rubbed at the corner of one eye, smudging her eyeliner into a blurry wing.

"Oh really?" Bo pressed, curious.

"It's our second home. Do you have a home here, too?"

Bo, amused now, shook her head and glanced around the room to try and track Michael. She barely made out Kurt and Mary as they swayed on the dance floor, blissfully unaware of the drama with their guests. Well, it was only Kurt she could see, thanks to his height. She assumed he was dancing with Mary.

Still no Michael in sight.

"You might know him, if you're a local," the woman said to Bo, bending closer to her now. Bo's body tensed and she pulled her credit card back in toward herself. Unease spread throughout her.

She looked again through the dark space, straining to catch a glimpse of Michael's gelled hair through the maze of cowboy hats and Texas-style bouffants. "Maybe," she answered, her focus shifting again to the barkeep.

"His name is Kurt Cutler."

———————

Bo's head swiveled like a top. "Excuse me?" She glanced around and brought a finger to her mouth and chewed on a nail as she finally met the woman's gaze.

"You know him?" An evil grin curled across her wet lips. Bo squinted up, dropped her hand, and stood, matching the woman's height. A memory smacked into her head. A rumor. Or gossip. Low-key drama of some sort. She heard about this woman. Months earlier.

Right when they had started dating, Mary called her sisters, frantic over a text she'd seen on Kurt's phone.

His ex-wife was in touch. Trying to get back together. Bo furrowed her brow, thinking hard about what had come to light.

"Sir," the woman called again to the bartender, who again ignored her. "Wow, service here sucks."

Bo struggled to recall exactly how things had shaken down, but she knew for a fact that Mary had resolved the matter. Kurt was divorced and had moved on. It wasn't a problem.

Looking out to the dance floor, she saw Kurt dip down, kissing Mary lightly before they pulled out of their embrace, about to leave the dance floor.

Urgency flooded Bo as she considered what to do. Trust Mary and Kurt? Kurt, especially? Believe he was really divorced? Believe he'd moved on and had no contact with this woman?

Or believe this woman, who'd rolled up to a Maplewood haunt all alone late at night on a holiday. Bo's eyes flashed back to Kurt, who was looking down at Mary as they slowly moved through the pack.

Something in Bo told her to handle the situation herself, without dragging poor Mary into the woman's drama.

On little more than a gut instinct, Bo grabbed the woman's arm and tore her away from the bar top, pushing roughly through the crowd along the far wall in order to avoid Kurt and Mary.

Confirming Bo's intuition, the woman did little more than giggle stupidly as she was dragged through the dark room and out into the chill of the mountain night.

Bo wasn't sure exactly what to say, but somewhere deep down, she knew she was making the right decision. Saving Mary, in some way. From humiliation or angst. At the very least from drama. Mary deserved better than to fall victim to a catfight at Last Chance.

Once they were outside, Brittany's ankle gave way and she toppled left. Bo caught her, righting her and giving her a good look under the yellow exterior light. The woman was clearly drunk.

"Did you drive up here from . . . Phoenix?" Bo squinted into her bleary eyes, wondering exactly who Kurt Cutler had married, and *why*.

She nodded her head and tears began to drop off her face, landing with little plunks on the pavement. "If Kurt thinks he can take ALL his money and move to Hicksville, then he's got another thing coming, 'cause he still loves me. I know he does," she slurred as the tears dried. She stumbled backward and leaned against the building. Bo glanced around her. They were alone out there. Now, flat against the logs of the bar's front entrance, even the back deck was invisible to them.

Bo narrowed her eyes on the wretched woman. "What's your name?"

"Brittany. Yours?"

"Brittany, I'm going to be honest with you. You're barking up the wrong tree being here. I am Kurt's fiancée's sister. You need to leave. In fact, I'll even drive you, since you're obviously plastered." Bo grabbed her arm and glanced around herself again, wondering what might become of Michael. Oh, well. He'd have to figure it out himself. She wasn't about to let this trashed piece of trash ruin Mary's night. Not after all of her sister's hard work on the party.

Brittany twisted her arm away from Bo, scraping her back along the wooden logs behind her and tumbling to the ground. "Get up," Bo demanded.

"What's going on out here?" A slick voice came up behind Bo, startling her. She turned, her eyebrows lifting in fear.

It was Michael.

Bo sighed in relief. "Hi, Michael. Um, well." She wasn't quite sure how much to explain. He shifted his eyes behind her to the lump of blonde on the walkway before pushing past Bo to grab the woman under her arms and pull her to her feet. Bo shrugged as Michael returned a confused gaze to her. "She's too drunk to drive."

Simple was best, Bo decided.

Brittany's eyes were closed and she rested her head on

Michael's shoulder. "I'll take her back to her place," he offered. His gaze leveled on Bo.

"She doesn't live here," Bo answered.

"Where does she live?"

Bo bit her lip, unwilling to open the can of worms to an almost stranger. "Phoenix. She's a . . . tourist."

Michael cleared his throat. "Is she staying at the lodge tonight? Is she Mary's guest?"

Bo shifted her weight. "No . . . well, yes." Dammit.

"I'll handle it, Bo. Can you go tell Kara I'm heading out? Maybe she can get a ride with you and the cop?"

Bo blinked, glancing behind her. "Keegan took Kara home," she answered as she turned back to him. "I mean back to the lodge. She needed to go to bed." Bo braced herself for his reaction, but she needn't have.

"I suppose Brittany should sleep it off, too, huh?" He repositioned himself under her weight and smiled at Bo.

A pit formed in her stomach as she realized just how bad a night this had become. Mary would be furious. Kurt, too, probably. But now, Bo was involved. She debated on whether to touch base with the others inside but quickly decided against it, opting instead to text Mary and Anna and give them the heads-up. Maybe they could cover her tab. She'd pay them back.

She'd fix it.

CHAPTER 8

Keegan noticed Kara was quiet on the ride to the lodge. But once they parked and she didn't move to unbuckle her seatbelt, Keegan turned to face her. "Everything okay?"

"Michael's been cheating on me."

She stared out the front windshield, her eyes apparently dry, hands folded in her lap. A total 180 degrees from the scene at the bar.

Keegan blew out a sigh and scratched his neck. He couldn't deal with this. He only went to the bar in order to be with Bo. Now, here he was, forced to play therapist to a total stranger who had a douchebag for a husband. He glanced back to her, killing the ignition and unbuckling his seat belt. "Kara," he began. She looked up, and he half-expected her to start sobbing. But instead, her face was impassive. Not sad. Not even angry. Dull, rather. He forged ahead, uncertain how to help. "Kara, if that's true, then you two need to work things out, somehow. But it's late. You've been drinking. I think the best thing to do right now is try to get some sleep. We can address it again in the morning, okay?"

He figured she'd fight that, insisting instead on crying it out, berating her husband as worthless. Maybe she'd even hit on Keegan. It had happened before. Not uncommonly.

But she didn't. She simply nodded, unfastened herself from the car, and pushed her way out, slowly trudging around the lodge to the back where the spare key sat waiting.

Minutes later, Keegan had let them in, moving behind Kara as she ascended the oak staircase up to the guest rooms. Once she had locked herself inside her room, he felt comfortable enough to head back down to wait for Bo.

It was past midnight by then, and Keegan was tired but awake. He had the next day off work, fortunately. And anyway, the chance at spending time with Bo kept him buzzing. For the time being, he settled into the long sofa anchored against the wall opposite the fireplace. The worn leather sank beneath him and he pulled out his phone to scroll mindlessly through news apps.

Twenty minutes later, a flood of warm light spilled through the front windows. He stood and crossed to the door, suddenly feeling uneasy for having left Bo with the responsibility of bringing Michael home, especially after Kara's revelation. He swallowed as he opened the door and crossed over the deck and down the steps, ready for trouble.

As he moved closer to Bo's vehicle, he noticed that it wasn't a man's figure sitting in the front seat. Yet, once the car was fully parked, Michael spilled out from the rear of the car.

Keegan walked faster toward him. "Hey, everything okay?"

Michael held up a hand. "Yes. One of Mary's guests turned up at the bar. Too much to drink is all. We're gonna get her to her room and call it a night. No big deal, man," Michael assured him. Keegan arrived at the car and opened the front door at the same time Bo opened hers.

In the seat sat a blonde woman slumped forward. Keegan threw a glance to Bo above the top of the car. Her hardened face gave away nothing.

He squatted down, finding himself surprised at the turn of events. As he reached his hands to shake her shoulders, she fell back in her seat, eyes closed, mouth agape. He didn't recognize her.

"When did she check in?" he asked as he moved back to a standing position. Bo looked away and Keegan turned his head to Michael. Something didn't add up.

Michael, for his part, also looked to Bo, who finally muttered, "Earlier today," before clapping her hands together and asking them to pull the limp body inside.

Keegan moved down to try and wake her, but her breaths came slowly and heavily. She was out cold. At last, he hoisted her out to Michael's waiting arms, and together, they walked her inside the cabin. For being as tall as she was, she was rail-thin and light as a feather.

Keegan shifted his weight cautiously beneath her left arm. They'd made it to the landing at the bottom of the stairs. Michael pulled the woman's body into his, holding her up effortlessly. Keegan looked at Bo. "Which room?"

CHAPTER 9

Bo licked her lips. The rooms were fully booked that night. There was no guest suite for Brittany. Unless . . .

"Room six," she answered and withdrew her own key from her pocket, gesturing upstairs. Her bed was made. Her personal belongings tucked neatly into her armoire. She'd carefully cleaned the space in preparation for the party. It would pass for an empty guest room. Her tidy nature paid off.

But now, everything had changed. And she needed to talk to Keegan. Privately. Before he left.

"Michael, can you take her up?" She didn't think he'd recognize the guest room was in fact her own personal room. She didn't care. Ever since Keegan had turned up at the party hours before, she wanted a moment alone with him. Several, in fact.

Bo's crush on Keegan began in high school, when she started dating his brother. In fact, the only reason she had dated Billy was to be closer to Keegan. Elusive, dark, edgy Keegan. The Flanagan brother who was least popular but, ironically, the hottest. Back then, his pale skin sat under a spray of freckles. A strong jawline and clear, bright eyes stood out from his Irish face and dark hair. Even then, he was built like a man—tall and muscular, deliciously proportionate. Strong. His refusal to participate in his younger brothers' antics endeared him to teachers but not to the cool crowd, unsurprisingly.

Keegan offered to help Michael with Brittany, but the stout architect masterfully slung the woman over his shoulder. Bo could read Keegan's mistrust, but she didn't care. She needed to talk to him. She *needed* him.

Once Michael was safely upstairs and in her bedroom with Brittany, Bo pulled Keegan to the back deck, where, in hushed whispers, she started at the beginning, describing her upsetting encounter with Kurt's ex and ending with her last-minute decision to give Brittany her bedroom, despite the unrest it was sure to cause.

"Kurt and Mary will flip out. She can't stay up there, Bo," Keegan reasoned, running a hand through his hair. "And you can't keep it a secret."

Bo paced the deck, walking the oak planks in nervous strides as Keegan crossed his arms and leaned against the railing. She chewed on a stubby fingernail and thought about Mary. Perfect Mary with her perfect life and perfect business. Perfect but innocent. Undeserving of this shit. Mary was the little sister who Bo never minded. She didn't get in the way. She'd always kept to herself. Then, at the beginning of senior year, their parents found a condom in Bo's backpack. The Delaneys were foaming with rage and threatened to make Bo leave the house for her final months of high school. They were ready to ship her off to a convent. Mary took up for her oldest sister, finding her tiny voice in a heated family argument. Bo could hear her sister's sweet words. *Bo has done more for this family than anyone else. She cooked for us and cleaned for us! She took us to school when you were too busy running the farm! You can't kick her out!*

The memory faded into the cool night. Bo's pace quickened. Keegan blew out a sigh.

"I could take her to a holding cell, but I'd have to write up a report. It might even make the papers, although you'd know more about that than me."

"No, no." Bo stopped and looked up at him. "We'll just let her sober up. When Mary and Kurt return, we won't say anything. We'll sneak her out in a few hours and drive her back to her car at Last Chance. She can figure it out from there."

"Bo," Keegan interrupted. "Wouldn't it make more sense to just tell Kurt and Mary? This is their business. Let them handle it."

Bo considered this for a moment. Technically, he was right. It wasn't her problem. She never should have involved herself, really. She licked her lips and resumed her pacing and nail-chewing as she thought through every possible course of action.

A. Text Mary. Tell her everything. Deal with Mary's reaction. And Kurt's. Compromise her relationship with both.

B. Keep Brittany a secret. Spare Mary the anguish. Say nothing. Sneak the woman out. Risk them finding out later and therefore compromise her relationship with them.

C. Keep Brittany a secret. Spare Mary the anguish . . . for now. Tell her later so that she can work through the issue with Kurt in their own way. Save the night. Earn more time with Keegan in the here and now.

That was it.

She turned on a heel and moved back to Keegan, her face flushing at what she was about to attempt. "Keegan, here's what we're gonna do." His eyebrows pinched together in confusion as she went through C, her solution. And before he could answer, she pushed up onto her toes, reached her hands behind his head, laced her fingers at the nape of his neck, and pressed her mouth into his, leaving behind all the stress of the night.

To her pure ecstasy, he returned the kiss in kind, his eyes falling shut, his mouth opening to accept her tongue, his hands pulling her waist into his.

The kiss lasted forever and momentarily. By the time she fell away from him, his eyes crept open. "I liked that." He grinned and flashed a glance behind her through the back windows into the great room of the lodge.

Bo followed his gaze, but no one was there. "Should you go check on her?" he asked, despite his firm grip on her waist.

"Hell, no," she spat. "That woman came here to break up my sister's engagement. She can sleep it off alone. I'm not babysitting her."

Keegan didn't argue, instead drawing her face back up to his and kissing her again.

Now, she wished she had left Brittany at the damn bar. She and Keegan could be in her bed right at this moment, taking this as far as she wanted. She could give in to temptation with someone good for once.

At the bar, Bo hadn't thought it through. Keegan was right. It was Mary's problem. Not hers. Dammit. But it was too late now.

Keegan fell back against the rail, moving his hands to her face, his fingers spread around her ears and into her hair. "Bo, I have had a crush on you forever," he admitted, searching her eyes.

She loved that he could let go of the circumstances and just be with her—in time and space. "Same here," was all she could answer as she twisted around, her mind wandering to when the others would return. She ought to check her phone. She ought to be responsible. But hadn't she already? Hadn't she been a good enough person that night? Taking on Mary's issue and fixing everything?

"Let's go for a walk." Bo grabbed Keegan's hand, laced her small fingers into his long ones, and led him down the back deck and out into the Adirondack chairs that framed the bonfire pit.

The area was off to the side of the lodge and out of sight from the rear windows. It was as much privacy as she could offer.

Playfully, she pushed him down into the chair. He sank in, his hand unhooking from hers as each of her legs slid around his hips and she eased onto his lap. Bo leaned down, her mouth pressing against his while he slipped his hands under the back of her shirt and stacked them on her spine, not daring to go any further.

Just then, the sound of tires crawling through gravel snapped the pair up from their prone position.

"What was that?" Keegan hissed. Bo let out a giggle.

"The others must be home." She pushed up off him and tiptoed through the gravel toward the lodge, looking for signs of movement. If the others were home, she didn't want to give up her position. She and Keegan had only begun.

Once she was satisfied that whoever had returned home was safely upstairs and not searching for her, she crept back over to Keegan, who was now standing next to the chair, his hands in his pockets.

Bo met his eyes, blushing faintly. "Coast is clear. Where were we?"

"There it is again," he whispered in the dark.

"Yeah, more than one car, remember?" She laughed quietly and pushed him back into the chair.

He grabbed her and pulled her down onto him, ready to finish what they had started.

CHAPTER 10

Eons passed as they rotated between kissing, whispering, and cuddling.

Keegan asked her why she was back in town. She said things didn't work out in Tucson and Mary needed the help. It was a win-win. He wondered if she was in town for good or if it was a stopover on her way to another gig. But he didn't ask.

Instead, Keegan changed the subject. "Who nick-named you Bo?" He asked, his voice low as he shifted under her weight. The night wasn't too cool yet, but with each breeze she shivered.

"I did."

He squinted down at the top of her head through the dark, amusement filling his face. "You nicknamed yourself?" He felt her nod against his chest. "You can't nickname yourself." He laughed quietly and nuzzled her head.

Bo sat up and faced him. Her clear eyes gleamed in the light of the moon. "Well I did, didn't I?"

He scratched his neck and lowered his chin, meeting her serious gaze. "How come?"

Bo sighed. "When Robbie was born I was like eight-years-old. I couldn't believe my parents named me Roberta and then him Robert. It was mortifying. Then, like a year later, I saw that movie. You know. *Ten*? With that blonde who had cornrows and a bangin' bod? I was at a friend's house and her parents were watching it on VHS. The dad was talking about the actress, Bo Derek. She was so beautiful. So that's what I chose."

Keegan wrapped a hand around the back of her head and pulled her into him, kissing her firmly. His mouth closed. Then he held her head against his for a moment. At last, she settled back down onto his chest. He felt her breaths grow slower. When he knew she was asleep, he whispered, "You are so beautiful, Roberta. Bo."

Exhaustion kicked in and sleep overtook Keegan, too.

———

Sometime later, Bo stretched awake, unpeeling her body from his and pulling out her phone to check the time.

Keegan yawned and did the same. It was just after three. "Should we see if Brittany barfed in your bed yet?"

She landed a playful punch on his arm before rubbing sleep from her eyes and offering a lazy grin. He took her hand and they moved back up the deck stairs where they cracked the door and slipped inside before pawing their way through the dark lodge.

As the two neared the stairs, Keegan peered out the windows in the foyer, searching to confirm Kurt and Mary and Anna and Dutch had safely returned to the lodge. The yellow glow of a front porch light illuminated the near-full parking lot, assuring him they indeed had.

A slow climb up the stairs taunted Keegan, and he forced himself to resist tucking a hand into the back pocket of Bo's jeans and cupping her soft, round butt.

Maybe, just maybe, they'd make it to the room and Brittany would be wide awake, regretful of landing herself there. Maybe she would thank them for taking care of her, assure them she had a different place to stay, and then promptly slip off into the night, leaving Bo's room empty and private for whatever kind of trouble he could stir up with the raven-haired Delaney.

As they reached the landing, Bo turned her head from side to side before glancing back at him and holding a finger to her lips. He followed her gaze as it settled on a room at the far right end of the hall. Together, they padded across a thick woven rug, pine floorboards creaking underneath the narrow carpet.

Bo held her hand back behind her and Keegan took it, lacing his fingers through hers.

At last they arrived at room number six. Above the placard was a wood engraving of a fox. Keegan liked the detail. It endeared him to the Delaney girls. He didn't know Mary terribly well, but she loved running her business on the mountain, where she grew up. She really embraced rural life, the lodge . . . Maplewood in general.

Bo had never seemed to. All she had really said about being back in town was that she nearly forgot just how crazy summer on the mountain could be.

She was right. After a few years of slow tourism, things

had finally turned around. That summer, Keegan's dad had said, the council predicted an influx of the local population from seven thousand to over twenty thousand. Sure enough, the projection proved valid, as Keegan found out personally. In June alone, his crew had recovered five camping parties who'd lost their way and one hiking party with a medical emergency. And that was just in Maplewood. The county search and rescue incidents were far higher and more varied. Everything from a missing teenager to several other adult disappearances since May.

Bo pushed a hand into her front pocket but looked up at him as she withdrew it, empty. "I gave it to Michael," she murmured, her tired eyes widening in alarm.

Keegan shrugged and whispered that he probably hadn't locked it and moved his own hand to the door, slowly turning the knob. Sudden panic filled the pit of Keegan's stomach. Should they have stayed with Brittany? How drunk was she? He knew better than to leave someone alone in that condition. His jaw tensed as he pushed the door open and air sucked them into the small room.

It was empty.

CHAPTER 11

Bo froze in the doorway before flying to the bathroom.

"Brittany?" she hissed as she grabbed the doorframe and pressed open the thick pine door.

Also empty.

Bo turned to Keegan, her eyebrows pinched, mouth agape. She closed it and glanced about the room as Keegan pulled the door shut.

"She must be here somewhere." Bo rubbed her eyes. Exhaustion had set in. Her body felt tingly and cold. All she wanted to do was slip into sweats and a hoodie and crawl under the covers—she didn't even care if Bimbo-Brittany-Used-To-Be-Cutler had drooled in her bed. She'd sleep on the floor if she had to.

She lifted her fingers off her eyelids and peered at Keegan, who ran a hand through his hair. "Well, we could check the house, if you want," he offered. "She might just be in someone else's room."

Bo shook her head. "What if Mary and Kurt found her?"

"Check your phone. They'd have texted you, right?"

She hadn't seen any messages before they came back in, but again, she pulled the phone from her pocket. Nope. She flashed the screen at him. Proof that he was wrong. He licked his lips and nodded. "Maybe she left," he suggested.

"How could she? No car, remember? She'd have had to walk through the woods to the highway. In the middle of the night? In a strange town? She's a psychobitch, but she isn't stupid."

He swallowed. "Let's walk the lodge and look. Maybe she's in the kitchen. Or she's sleeping on the couch and we missed her."

Bo let out a sigh. "Fine, okay, yeah." It had to be the wildest night of her life, and that was saying something. Her interest in Keegan shuffled itself to the backseat. All she could hope for now was to find Brittany, deposit her in a motel, and call it a night. Things with Keegan could resume in the morning, after sleep and a shower.

They crept back out of the room, taking care not to lock the door, and then down the staircase. Keegan tapped on the flashlight feature of his phone and shone it across the lower level of the lodge.

A scan of the reception area revealed nothing more than long shadows pooling out from behind the scant furnishings.

They moved into the great room, where they'd just crossed through. As light yellowed the leather, no shape appeared, human or otherwise. Just tufted cowhide.

Bo felt like a character in Scooby-Doo as they ventured

from the great room into the kitchen on their tiptoes, backs hunched.

Nothing.

Dining room . . . Nothing.

Downstairs bath . . . Nothing.

All clear. Keegan killed the flashlight and reached an arm around Bo's shoulders, rubbing briskly up and down. He, too, must have caught a chill.

"We have to wake Michael," Keegan hissed through the darkness.

Bo whispered back, "Why?"

"He saw her last. He put her in the room."

Bo nodded even as a sinking feeling of guilt gnawed at the pit of her stomach.

They climbed back up the staircase, and fear prickled along her spine as they hovered outside room seven. The carved timber wolf gazed at her as she held a fist up to rap on the door.

She waited a beat, then dropped her hand, turning to Keegan and pressing her palms on his taut chest and pushing past him, away from the door, and toward the railing. He held his phone at his waist, its screen glowing up on his face. A shadow passed over his eyes, and his brow furrowed but he joined her at the railing.

"What's wrong?" He asked.

She pushed up on her toes and brought her mouth to his ear. "I can't do it." She fell back down. "What if we wake the other guests? Not just Mary or Anna or Kara. What about the *real* guests?" Her mind flashed to the innocent college kids who'd irritated her the day before.

Oh, if only they were the main hassle. She could put up with loud-mouthed party kids.

She couldn't put up with a pissy wife. She *really* couldn't put up with a missing stranger. "Keegan, I can't do it."

He grabbed the back of her head and pressed his lips to the side of her face. "You have to."

She frowned and mouthed back breathlessly. "Kara's going to flip out. Cause a scene. Wake the whole lodge."

Keegan hooked a hand around her waist and moved her to the side before striding up to the door and lightly thudding with his middle knuckle.

The sound echoed against the silence of the hallway, rattling Bo awake. She wrapped her arms around herself, glancing side to side. She half-expected a robe-and-slippers-clad Mary to swing her door open, hands on hips. *What's going on out here?* Her voice would ring throughout the pre-dawn air of the lodge.

A slit formed in the doorjamb. Bo and Keegan involuntarily stepped back, uncertain what to expect. The wooden door slowly fell open, revealing Michael's sleep-worn face in its gap. Bo tried to peer beyond him into the black room, but Michael quickly squeezed out, taking care to close the door behind him without a sound.

He scratched the back of his head before moving his hand to rub his eyes. They instantly perked and he asked, "Is everything okay?"

Keegan cleared his throat and motioned Michael to follow him toward the stairs. Bo kept close to Keegan as they descended into the great room. The glow from Keegan's phone coupled with that of the front porch light aided their journey to the fireplace, where Bo spun around. Now, relieved that neither Mary nor Kara were aware of anything, she took back control from Keegan. "Michael, Brittany's gone?" Her voice a low hiss, it came out like a question.

Michael's eyes flashed and he glanced behind him. Again, he scratched the back of his head, then rubbed his eyes. In the dim light, Bo saw his tongue jab out between his lips before he swallowed. She looked up to Keegan, whose eyes were steady on the squat architect.

Finally, Michael answered. "She woke up right after you two went downstairs. I sat with her for a while before she called a cab . . . or a car, I guess. She left." He cleared his throat and glanced behind him and up the stairs.

Bo began to reply, but Keegan clasped her shoulder hard, halting her. His eyes remained level on Michael, who was now fidgeting with the buttons on his crisp, flannel pajamas. He looked like a cartoon dad on vacation.

Michael swallowed again. "Okay, okay. Listen, I don't want Kara to know I was with Brittany." He rubbed his hand down his face, drawing his eyebrows over his eyes. "She'll flip. We're going through some shit right now, and I don't need it. I was just trying to help." His hand moved to the back of his neck again and he twisted to look up the stairs.

Bo didn't want a scene, either. And it was a plausible explanation for his behavior. "Where did the car take her? Who was driving?" As if Bo even cared.

"She's, ah, she's staying at a motel near the town square. I guess she found a number for a private driver. She walked out on her own. I'm sure she's fine. Just needed to sober up." Michael had crossed his arms over his chest and relaxed somewhat.

Keegan loosened his grip from Bo's shoulder then dropped his hand to hers, giving her a gentle squeeze. "Bo?"

She looked up at him, uncertain what he wanted.

"Sound right to you?"

Bo looked back at Michael whose eyebrows crumpled together. Heavy bags hollowed beneath his eyes. It was the look of a man in a crap marriage. Not that she knew. All Bo wanted was to keep the whole thing quiet and tuck herself into bed. She'd be better off dealing with it in the morning after a pot of coffee.

She nodded up at Keegan. "I'm wiped. Let's call it a night."

The somber trio ascended the staircase for the last time that night.

Once Bo and Keegan returned to her room, she stripped the bed and threw a fresh sheet and blanket over top. She and Keegan fell into the bed with little more than murmured *goodnights*.

CHAPTER 12

Though it had been only three hours since he'd conked out, Keegan woke with a start at six a.m. There was no bucking his routine, even under serious sleep deprivation. He sprang awake in Bo's bed, his head pounding and mouth dry. He glanced over at her on the mattress beside him.

Had High-School-Keegan known this was in his future, he'd have socked himself in the face for not sealing the deal.

The blanket had bunched between them, and Keegan untangled it before draping it carefully over Bo, who lay face-down, purring like a cat through strands of her midnight hair. He swung his legs over the side of the bed and stood, stretching his long, lean body. He pulled his phone from his jeans pocket. Dead.

Didn't matter. It was the day after the Fourth. He wasn't on duty. Or on call. He was a free man.

A free man who desperately needed coffee and felt

incredibly uncomfortable making himself at home in Mary's lodge.

He had no choice but to head home, grab a quick shower, hit lame-ass JavaTime, and return.

Glancing around the room, he looked for a piece of paper and pen to leave a note. All that appeared was one of Mary's brochure packets and a pen on the side table. He found some white space between ads for the *Mountain Times* and his own mother's real estate business.

Uncertain if she'd even see it, he scrawled quickly, leaving the brochure on top of the sheet next to her.

Wild night. Be back with coffee. -K

———

As he drove, his radio crackled to life, dispatch officers knee-deep in a back-and-forth with one or two cops. Silencing the radio, he thought back to Bo. The curve of her back in the bed. Her wild hair splayed across the pillow and across her face. Her full lips. On his.

Minutes later, he pulled up to his house, killed the engine, jogged inside, tethered his phone for a quick charge, and jumped into a cold shower to rinse off. After grabbing his towel and patting off beads of water, he brushed his teeth and dressed in fresh jeans and a white tee.

Soon enough, he was back in the truck, phone in his pocket, as he peeled out of his drive and back toward the highway.

It was half past six, and Keegan wanted to make it back

to the lodge by seven. He realized he wasn't entirely sure how many guests he ought to get coffee for. Just Bo? The whole lodge? Bo had mentioned a booked house, which meant at least ten or so folks.

"Party jug, please," he relayed to the window clerk, who promptly directed him to pull into a spot to give them time to make a fresh carafe and fill a boxed jug.

It gave him time to scan over the phone activity he'd missed from the early hours of the day. No doubt updates on tourist antics from the night before.

The first missed call, however, was from his dad. He never heard from his dad. It was more typically his mom who would text with dinner invites or to pry about his weekend exploits.

He tapped the icon to return his dad's call, instantly converting it to speaker in order to read through the rest of the missed texts.

But his dad gave him no chance.

"Keegan? Where the hell have you been?" Keegan began to answer, confused and concerned. But his father interrupted him. "Have you heard? Did they call you in yet?"

"No, Dad, what are you talking about? Slow down, jeez."

"Is he okay?" His mom's voice wafted through the phone, alerting him to the fact that he, too, was on speaker.

Keegan blew out a sigh and checked his rearview for a steaming cardboard jug. No luck, yet. "I'm fine, Mom. Dad, what's up?"

"A woman was reported missing. Two days ago. Phoenix put out an APB. County just got hold of it yesterday."

A faint memory tugged on Keegan's brain. He was vaguely familiar with the news. But as of yesterday afternoon, there was no formal bulletin for Navajo County. He began to scroll through his texts, catching a couple from another deputy and an alert from work. His dad launched into the rest of his news just as Keegan read it on his phone.

"Her credit card got a hit at a gas station outside of town near the canyon. They think she was on her way up here from Scottsdale."

A pit grew in the bottom of Keegan's stomach.

Kurt Cutler was from Scottsdale.

He knew he had to come forward with the events of the night before.

He closed his eyes and pressed a thumb into each eyelid as his dad paused on the other end. Finally, Keegan sighed. *Shit*. "Dad, what's the name of the missing woman?"

"Purcell."

Keegan breathed. A rap came at his window, and he jumped, nearly dropping his phone.

"Dad, hang on."

He accepted the coffee and a stack of insulated paper cups, all of which he balanced on his passenger seat before returning to the phone and throwing the truck into reverse.

His mother's voice came nearer to the speaker. "They

think she was driving up here to track down her old boyfriend or something."

Keegan felt his heart skip a beat. The coincidence was undeniable now. But . . . Purcell?

"What else do you know?" He was stupid to ask them when he could just as easily pick up the phone and call the chief, who'd fill him in. But stalling would at least take him to the lodge, where he could see Bo one last time before he had to report to the station. Report what he knew.

What he did.

His parents bickered in hushed tones before Bob Flanagan came back over the phone. "Keegan, the woman is Kurt Cutler's ex-wife."

———

Keegan had nearly crashed the truck. He forced himself to breathe, hanging up on his father without a word.

The smartest thing to do would be to call his boss.

But he had to talk to Bo first.

Arriving at the lodge felt different now. Last night, it shone like a beacon of hope. Now, it loomed like a haunted house.

He parked the truck and sat for a moment, carefully reading through the messages he'd previously skimmed. Everything his dad said was confirmed except for the name. Missing Scottsdale woman. APB Apache County. Thought to have stopped at Old Towne Gas and Goods. Connected to a part-time resident. All deputies report for duty ASAP.

He scratched the stubble along his jaw and tapped out a reply to Carl, his closest friend on the force.

Phone died. On my way. Get me a mtg with chief pronto. I have info.

He jogged to the front door of the lodge and alternated between ringing the bell and knocking. He wasn't quite sure how to handle this, but it was urgent, so it didn't matter if he woke the whole house. They'd find out in no time anyway.

He pressed his face to the window, waiting for someone—anyone—to descend the staircase. Soon enough, the flash of a robe caught his eye. Mary. She floated down the steps and to the door, opening it quietly but quickly. Fear struck her face. "Keegan, hi. Are you okay?"

He shoved the coffee at her and murmured a quick "Yes, 'scuse me, ma'am," before bounding up the stairs to Bo's room and hammering on her door.

Mary was hot on his heels, cutting left down the hall and moving into her room to get Kurt.

Bo finally answered before the other doors started cracking open.

"Where were you?" she asked, her eyes wild.

"Follow me." He grabbed her hand and waved at the curious onlookers, addressing them professionally. "There's been an incident. I need to talk to Bo. Just stay here."

Once they were outside on the front deck, he spoke in fast, hushed tones, explaining to her exactly what he knew and his plan: he would report to the station. She could come if she wanted. Regardless, her sisters and their dates and Michael and Kara had to stay at the lodge. He was in full-on cop mode, now.

Her response came as no surprise. "Let's go. I'm ready."

He glanced behind her through the windows as Mary and Anna watched them from the reception desk.

"We have to tell your sisters."

"Okay," she began as she turned to go in.

He grabbed her. "I will."

He pulled open the door and fell into a briefer version of what he'd delivered to Bo. "Mary, Anna. There's been a missing person's report. There's a chance, just a chance, the woman involved was here last night."

His revelation resulted in gasps from the bare-faced sisters. They began to speak but he held up a hand. "I can't get into details. Bo is joining me at the station. I'll have her send word when we know more. Could be a false alarm."

With that, he turned and grabbed Bo by the elbow, guiding her out to the truck as she darted a look to Mary and Anna.

They buckled themselves into the truck and he took off down the lane and toward the highway. Bo was quiet. Tense.

Just as they turned left to head into town, a fresh crackle blared forth from his radio. The dispatcher's voice calm and clear.

"Squad 928 to Zick Ranch Road East. Hogtown. We've got a 10-54 at the lake out there by Logan Zick's place. Over."

Bo glanced to Keegan, whose knuckles had grown white on the steering wheel. "What's a 10-54?"

He swallowed hard, his eyes on the road as he swerved into the right lane, not bothering to check his mirror. Their route had just changed.

"Dead body."

CHAPTER 13

Brittany had awoken with a headache. A throbbing ache that began in the base of her skull and stretched its tentacles into the back of her eye sockets.

Three things occurred to her.

1. She never found Kurt.
2. Michael was married. Shit.
3. She didn't know where she was.

Brittany shifted in her seat, confused at having passed out again. There, inside, a light buzzed overhead, casting its yellow glow over the purse that slumped on her lap. She peered out her window into pine trees and blackness.

Nothing cut through the night. No sound nor sight.

Shifting again, Brittany twisted around, and her gaze fell on the bench behind her. A tarp loomed high, its crinkly form tented above her eye level.

Footsteps cut through the silence. Thuds cracking

twigs and scuffing through pine needles. Brittany reached a hand to lift the corner of the tarp.

A voice crackled through her window. "You're awake." She twisted back in her seat and nodded at the dark figure.

"Had to stop for a minute. Let's get back to it." Again, she nodded and then stole another glance back at the tarp before the figure disappeared and reappeared in the seat behind her. "Mind your damn business."

CHAPTER 14

Bo had never seen a dead body before.

She'd seen dead chickens. Dead dogs. Dead pigs. Never a dead human.

As soon as they descended from Keegan's truck, her eyes narrowed on the bloated flesh peeking out from folds of soaked fabric just yards away.

Nausea hollowed her stomach, and she steadied herself against the hood of Keegan's truck as he strode away from her and toward the uniforms working the scene.

Keegan huddled himself against a notebook-wielding man, and Bo took in the scene. A smattering of people combed the area, some hunched and examining the shoreline. Techs in plastic suits worked the body, which Bo forced herself to ignore. She couldn't afford to launch into dry heaves. She probably shouldn't even be there.

As her eyes drifted toward the old fisherman's house that sat at the end of the dock, she scanned the area for Old Man Zick.

Logan Zick was the stuff of legends. Bo had met him a

handful of times in town, but it was his brothers she really knew. After all, she worked for them.

In fact, Mary, the only Delaney sister who stuck around town, knew Logan better than Bo. She even recalled that Mary had brought Kurt down here for a date a few months back. Ice fishing.

The water must still be cold. It's not like Maplewood saw scorching temps, even in the dead of July.

Just as she was about to tear her gaze away from the run-down shack, a roar broke out from beyond it. Old Man Zick was striding ahead of a cop, who had begun to jog after him. Swears and spittle flung themselves from the geezer's toothless mouth. The commotion spilled over his dirt driveway and toward Keegan and the detective. Dust kicked up around the crusty, old fisherman as he flailed a finger toward the engorged body.

"Get that damned roadkill off my damned property, you son-of-a-wench city boy, before I do it my own self, for God's sake."

The detective shook his head and held up a hand. "We're not going anywhere, Mr. Zick. I don't care how upset you are. This is a death investigation, and we intend to work it to a satisfying conclusion."

The lecture served only to enrage Logan further. "What the hell kind of investigation you boys gon' do out here? Damned body floated up in *my* lake. That's called *trespassing* in case you ain't familiar with the *law*. And what's more, it's contaminating *my* fish. No doubt I won't be able to offload the little assholes for months. In fact, I'm goin' to sue the shit out of everyone. Trespassing and contamination. If you wanna investigate why that Barbie bitch over there threw her drunk ass into my moneymaker, then have at it. Ain't no evidence here gonna tell you that, though. Why not go dig up her friends who're no doubt still drunk off their asses in town? And while you're at it, this seems like the perfect opportunity to close the roads. Summer's over. No more got-damned *tourists*." He finished his piece with a hearty spit toward the lake.

Under other circumstances, Bo would sympathize with Logan.

"Get this old fool up to the station and book him for interference," the detective directed, dismissing him like a gnat.

The cop who'd been trailing Logan grabbed his hands and cuffed him in record time, leaving no chance for the miser to wriggle free and haul off at someone. Just as he was shoved toward a cruiser, a red SUV pulled up and crunched itself over pine needles.

Out hopped Paul Zick. Bo's breath caught in her throat.

"Calm the hell down, e'r'body. My big-shot brother just shown up and y'all are gon' be real sorry."

Paul crossed to Logan and the cop who wrestled him into the back seat. They exchanged brief words before the calmer Zick man strode over to the detective and Keegan.

"You the one who called us?" the detective asked.

"Yeah. Yes. So sorry about Logan. He's . . ." Paul twirled a finger around his head before his gaze caught on Bo.

The detective followed Paul's gaze and pointed at her. "And who the hell is this?"

Bo licked her lips, the nausea ebbing and converting

into a fight response. She pushed off the hood of Keegan's trunk and stuck out her hand.

"Bo Delaney. At your service."

He squinted from Paul to Keegan and back to Bo.

Bo looked at Paul, realizing his participation here had nothing to do with the paper. But hers very well could. The first line to a paper-selling article wrote itself across her brain and she forced a smile down.

"You and you, outta here." The detective pointed at Keegan and Bo. "We don't need any more men on the scene. Pack it in." The detective waved them back, gesturing to Keegan's truck.

"Dawson," Keegan stopped him. "We might have info on the case."

The man dropped his hand and let out a sigh. "Oh, yeah? Why didn't you start with that?"

Keegan stuck his hands in his pockets and Bo peered around him toward the body, desperate for any confirmation on the identity or details she might cook up in a report. If they'd let her write one.

After all, she might be on the other side of that article if things didn't go well. A shudder wracked her body and she glanced back to Keegan and Dawson before returning her focus to the body. She was about to lose her opportunity to take it all in. She had to look. She had to see.

The body was on its side. Hands tied behind the back and to the ankles. Matted, muddy hair clumped against the scalp. The skin of the arms and legs was swollen and bruised. Or perhaps mud-caked. It was impossible to tell. Despite the excessive bloating of the body, the woman's shirt clung to her breasts and lifted away from her stomach, offering no modesty.

A tarp floated over the body and techs stood above her head, eyeing Bo as they wrapped up their work.

The detective held his radio to his mouth. "Biggans, what's your twenty?"

A garbled voice answered and Dawson whistled for a uniform to join them. Keegan nodded in solemn recognition to the young cop whose face lit up.

"Keegan effin' Flanagan, how you been, man? Haven't seen you since that hiking case. Man, Search and Rescue was all over the girl early this morning. I figured we'd run into each other. Have you seen her? Rough, man. Real rough."

Dawson interjected. "Flanagan and his, uh, *friend* have information on the case. They need to make a formal statement. Can you take them back to the station and get it rolling?"

The younger guy's mouth parted and his eyes grew wide. He took a quick moment before agreeing. "Yeah, let's do it. Are we . . . Are you taking your truck, or?"

Dawson began to answer. "No, they'll go with you."

Keegan shook his head. "We'll follow in the truck. Don't you worry about us, Dawson."

The men exchanged a steely look, but Bo knew Keegan didn't have to suffer fools. He was a county sheriff. Son of the mayor. Maplewood golden boy. This Dawson character had no way of enforcing the laws of the land on Keegan. He was safe.

Bo hoped she was, too.

Once they were in the truck and on the road, Bo cleared her throat.

"Doesn't he know who you are?"

Keegan's expression didn't soften. "I should have had my phone on. I missed the APB this morning. They had a lead on this girl as early as four or five a.m. I dropped the ball, Bo."

She flushed. A lame apology formed in her head.

Instead, Bo pulled her phone from her pocket and began to chew on a nail. Three unread texts from Mary.

Visions of the previous night fluttered through her head. She and Keegan were undoubtedly implicated, assuming the dead body was Brittany Purcell-Cutler.

But Bo and Keegan weren't the last to see Brittany.

Tears welled in Bo's eyes as she tapped out a reply to her little sister.

Try not to worry. Just keep everyone there at the lodge. Make sure you stay together. We're going to the station now. Don't freak out. I'll get back to you ASAP.

She knew it was alarmist. But this was an alarming situation.

After all, her sisters could be drinking coffee with a murderer.

CHAPTER 15

"Keegan, a word?"

Bob Flanagan cupped his son's elbow and whisked him back outside into the bright morning sun, leaving Bo to sit in the waiting area with Detective Biggans.

Keegan's stomach lurched from hunger and nerves. A dull throb had begun to swell at the base of his head. When he'd arrived at Mary's party the night before, he had a dramatically different picture of what the worst-case scenario could be, and it involved thwarted advances on Bo, not a heavy make-out session followed by the discovery of a dead tourist. A dead tourist who may or may not have spent the night in Bo's room.

"Dad, is she Kurt's ex?" He still hadn't received official confirmation.

"They haven't ID'd the body yet. It might be Brittany. Listen, we can bring a lawyer in at any time. No sense in playing the hero here. I've got you covered, okay?" His dad pinned him with a meaningful look.

Keegan shrugged the man off. Bob Flanagan was

worried about covering his own ass. Keegan was worried about finding a killer.

As soon as Keegan and his dad returned inside, Biggans put it all on the line. "Mayor, I'll have to take Keegan into a separate room from Miss Delaney."

Bob began to protest, but Keegan waved him off and followed Biggans to the back.

Soon enough, he was sitting on the wrong side of a metal table whose chair was not-so-discreetly chained to the floor. Biggans left a pen and paper and asked Keegan to jot down whatever info he had. The detective would return shortly.

Once he was back, Keegan slid the paper across the table and tossed the pen on top. "Brady, listen." He didn't know Brady Biggans well, but he was familiar enough. Unlike Logan Zick, Keegan didn't mind that much of the force wasn't from the mountain. It gave them an edge. A distance. And those things were important to quality police work. But Brady Biggans wasn't going to have a quality investigation if he wasted time here with Keegan and Bo.

Brady grabbed for the paper and Keegan continued. "Here's the deal, man. Bo and I linked up at Last Chance. Her sisters and their dates were there. So was another couple. Friends of the family, I guess. Michael and Kara. Bo'll know their last name. Kara got drunk off her ass, and I offered to drive her home. Bo stayed back to get Michael."

He paused and took a sip from the paper cup on the table. By now, Biggans had eased himself into the adjacent chair and leaned back to listen.

"Soon enough, Bo shows up at the lodge with Michael and this mystery woman who, like Kara, was out of it. According to Bo, this woman says she's Kurt Cutler's ex. We wanted to spare the drama, let her sleep it off. Michael carried her upstairs, and that's the last we saw of her, Brady. When we went up to check on her some time later, she was long gone. Michael said she called a car service and headed down to one of the motels."

Keegan took another sip, letting the events settle over the detective before finishing his spiel. "So, here's what you're gonna do, Brady. You're gonna call every tourist trap motel, hotel, bed-and-breakfast, guest house, second home, and so on and so forth. Meanwhile, you're gonna call every car service on the mountain. And," Keegan went on, hardly stopping for a breath, "you're gonna question every person who was at the Last Chance beginning with Michael, the cheating architect."

CHAPTER 16

Once she left the room, Bo felt even worse. Learning that the dead woman could be Brittany Cutler was just the tip of the iceberg. The cop told her to stay in town and make herself available. She had never in her life been in this kind of trouble.

However, it wasn't the trouble that maddened her. It was that the cop obviously didn't believe her.

Bo told him everything from A to Z, sparing no detail. She even described how she and Keegan hooked up on an Adirondack chair behind the lodge. Bo was of the opinion that in murder cases, there was no such thing as too few details, even if it behooved her to keep it simple.

And while she didn't want to cast unnecessary suspicion on Michael, she clearly indicated that he was the last person to see Brittany at the lodge. The next person after Michael would have been whoever gave her a ride to the motel. And then on down the line until someone knew *something*.

After an hour and a half of questions and walking

through the night, she was released conditionally. As she walked from the sterile room and into the white-walled hall, she caught sight of a water fountain and her thirst returned with a vengeance. She pulled her hair back with one hand, bent over the aluminum box, and sucked in a long slurp of cool water before wiping her mouth with the back of her hand and straightening. Then she strode out to the waiting area where Bob Flanagan paced, his phone glued to his ear.

Keegan was nowhere to be seen, so she took a seat and listened in on the mayor's convo.

"Hun, I'm tellin' ya, it's a one-and-done deal over here . . . Yeah, I just talked to Detective Dawson. One body. Dead as a doornail. Definitely an out-of-towner . . . Press release? Well, hell yeah, we have to give a statement, Victoria. I wasn't born yesterday . . . I dunno, why don't you work it up and send it to Lisa . . . Well then, why the hell'd you call if you're so busy, Victoria? Murder in Maplewood is big news in case you didn't realize."

With that, he stabbed at the phone and muttered a curse before stabbing again and returning it to his ear. His face glowing red, an excitability coursed through him and he paced to the far end of the hall, now lowering his voice.

Just then, Keegan walked out of the restroom. Bo smoothed her hair and stood, taking in the sight of him. His shoulders back, Keegan's tall body showed no signs of the fear that had been eating at her all morning. His face gave no indication of the sleep deprivation from which they both suffered. His lips were full and smooth. His eyes bright.

Crossing to her, he wrapped an arm around Bo's shoulders and bent his head down to hers. "It's not looking good."

Her eye twitched and she pushed back, staring up at him. "What's that mean?"

Keegan grabbed her hand and led her from the building, waving casually to his father and the receptionist at the desk as they pushed through the front door. Once they were outside in the warm sun, she stopped, tugging his hand. "What do you mean, Keegan?"

He dropped her hand and ran his fingers through his hair. "I'm on leave. Effective immediately and for the duration of the investigation or until you and I are cleared completely."

Bo's face fell.

Any romantic opportunity with Keegan slipped through her fingers. It was obvious he cared about his career. His reputation. Both of which were at stake.

She was to blame. She crossed her arms over her chest and looked away as she bit down on her lip, willing herself to keep it together.

After all, it wasn't the missed love connection that bothered her the most.

It was her unmissed connection to a murder. Or, at the very least, to a missing person's case. She could set aside for a minute that there was a very dead woman rotting on the shore of Hogtown Lake. She couldn't, however, set aside the coincidence of her sister's fiancé's ex-wife going missing on the mountain *and* a dead woman turning up. When would they find out if it was Brittany? How slowly did these things happen?

Keegan's arms wrapped around her again and

pulled her close. She felt him press his lips on the top of her head. Did her hair smell like cigarette smoke and beer? Here she was, in the arms of the guy she'd swooned over since she was a stinky little kid, and she probably smelled just the same—like a stinky little kid.

And he was still hugging and kissing her. Maybe everything would be okay. Maybe.

Without warning, she tore back from him and dug her phone out of her pocket. "Hang on a sec," she muttered breathlessly as she opened the only new message. It was her sister.

Police just showed up. Everyone heading in for questioning. Do we know the missing girl???

Bo bucked up and answered the text truthfully, though she figured Mary was already en route. Maybe in the back of a police car. Weary, she rubbed her eyes and felt the prick of tears flood her lower lash line. "Keegan, what are we going to do?"

But before he could respond, her eyes grew wide and her heartbeat quickened. She looked again at her phone. "Wait! Oh, no! The office. I was supposed to work today. Shit!" She grabbed his hand and dragged him to his truck where he followed her directions down to the Podunk offices of the *Mountain Times*.

"Bo, I'm sure they'll understand if you can't make it in today." He glanced over from his spot behind the steering wheel. She felt him stare at her messy hair and makeup-smudged face.

Wiping at the corners of her eyes, she returned his gaze. "No, I have an idea. I'm going to do a write-up." Bo swallowed, fully expecting him to shut her down. Obviously it was a conflict. But *what* a great story.

Local reporter finds herself ensnared in murder case. She's freed from jail in time to share her side of the case . . .

Electricity buzzed through her veins. Excitement replaced her fears and anxieties, and she allowed it to.

For over fifteen years of writing for newspapers, Bo Delaney had never been inspired. Never interested. Never *invested*.

Now, here, Bo found herself. Smackdab in the middle of a murder case. If that wasn't inspiration, then she didn't know what was. All those restless years of writing about nonsense. Pop-up food trucks. Skorts making a comeback. They had dulled her senses. But now, her fear coalesced into something more: motivation. Motivation for writing a piece with grit and substance. It was her chance.

Those damn, useless tourists had something to offer the mountain, after all. Or, at least, they had something to offer Bo.

As soon as gravel crunched under their tires, Bo bolted from the truck and into the office.

"Is Stewart here?" She threw the question out into the air as soon as she entered, but no one was around to hear her. She paused, listening for murmuring.

The conference room.

She dashed down the hall, feeling Keegan behind her opening the door. As she twisted the knob and pushed her way in, four rapt expressions turned on her. Staff meeting.

Stewart's mouth froze open as he took in the bedraggled reporter who normally functioned barely above the level of acceptable work ethic and output. Bo flipped into action. "I know, I know. I've hardly slept, okay? Listen, Stewart. I have to talk to you about something."

Stewart Zick was one of Paul's four brothers. He acted as assistant editor-in-chief, which was blatant nepotism. Didn't matter. Nepotism was much the fabric of a small town. A staple, really.

Two of the other Zick brothers were town drunks. The third, of course, was also a drunk. But Logan insisted he lived *out* of town, despite being a stone's throw from Wood Smoke Lodge and the rest of Maplewood's north end.

All eyes flashed to Stewart, whose face crinkled in confusion. "Aren't you . . . Weren't you at the station?" He cleared his throat and grabbed a sip from his thermos. "Lionel, take over here while I chat with Roberta."

Bo cringed but waited patiently for him to join her in the hallway, where Keegan stood, hands in pockets.

Stewart's eyes narrowed on Bo. "You can't be here, Roberta. Not while you're waist-deep in a murder investigation."

She propped her hands on her hips. "Obviously I'm not waist-deep or I wouldn't be standing here with you. If anyone is waist-deep, it's your brother, who's at the crime scene as we speak. And anyway, what would make a better story than a reporter who is on the inside of it?" Bo held his gaze, wondering exactly how Stewart or Paul could ignore the big fat gift that just plopped in the paper's lap: her involvement in the murder. Assumedly.

He sighed and looked to Keegan. "It's a conflict of interest. Integrity is a founding principal of our publication. We can't bend morals for a juicy story."

Bo pressed ahead and past his generic hypocrisy. "I

understand that. I do. But if we are going to offer investigative journalism for our customers . . . for our *community*, then we better investigate this case. And if you want the truth, then you'll let me write it."

Stewart considered her plea, rubbing his chin and peering out the window at the front of the office.

Bo felt him growing distracted and followed his gaze. Walking in through the door was Mayor Flanagan. Bo glanced back to Stewart, who began to nod. "Okay, once you're cleared with one hundred percent certainty, then we'll talk. We'll ask Paul. For now, you can't be here." He lifted his chin toward the mayor.

"Hi Stewart, how ya been doin'?" The put-upon drawl turned Bo's stomach and she stepped aside to watch as Keegan awkwardly stood there, his hands still stuffed in his pockets. "Keegan, Roberta, how ya doin'?"

Keegan nodded to his dad before sliding one hand down to hers and lacing their fingers. Her heart leapt at the public show of affection and she followed him to the waiting area, leaving the two men to speak privately.

Bo kept her ears open as she and Keegan walked off, but they kept mum, their eyes trained on the back of her head.

She could feel it.

CHAPTER 17

As they stepped outside, Keegan felt Bo pull away. "What was your dad doing there?" she pressed.

He shook his head. He had no idea. He also felt the rumble of hunger grow in his stomach. "Wanna grab a bite?"

Bo agreed and they took off to Darci's, where coffee and toast revived them somewhat. Darci's was *the* place to be for breakfast and brunch, which forced the two to keep a low profile and remain mum.

She mostly scrolled on her phone and picked at the skin around her nails. He could tell she was desperate to hear from her sisters. Know that they were okay. He also knew that on a normal day he'd be able to pull a few strings and get insider info from the station.

Today wasn't normal, though.

Once they'd finished, he paid the bill and they jumped back in the truck. "Where to?" He asked.

"I'm so worried about Mary." She dodged his question, so he sat with the engine idling as she chewed on her lower lip. "I mean, I know she will be absolved. And so will Kurt. And Anna and Dutch, too, of course. But this whole thing sucks. Oh my God, Keegan. A murder. What if she was killed in my bedroom?"

The morbid thought had already crossed his mind, turning sour his earlier romantic notions of seducing Bo in that bedroom. Crime scene or not, it was forever tainted. Wood Smoke Lodge was forever tainted. He wondered what would become of it after things settled. Even if Brittany wasn't killed there, it would forever carry a stigma. The haunted lodge of Maplewood Mountain.

He threw the truck in reverse and pulled out of Darci's, taking a right onto the highway.

Bo stared out the window. "I need a shower."

Minutes later, they were passing Maplewood Lake and rolling into Keegan's drive. Bo hadn't uttered a word. Not even a question about where they were. Her head was now leaning on the window. He reached a hand over, brushing a strand of hair behind her ear. She didn't stir.

"Bo?" he whispered through the cab of his truck. He cut the engine and the sound of ducks and geese replaced its hum. "Bo?" He raised his voice, but she seemed to slink further away. He leaned forward and saw both her eyes were closed, her mouth parted, rhythmically letting out light breaths. She'd fallen fast asleep.

He quietly let himself out of the truck and jogged around the front to her side, where he cracked the door until he was confident she wouldn't fall right out. Once he had it open, he tried one last time. "Bo? Wake up, Bo. We're here."

Her breaths were deeper now and even. So, he slid one

hand beneath her thighs and the other behind her back and lifted her out in one swift motion. Just as he swung her body out of the car, she woke with a start.

"Where are we?"

He set her down as she rubbed the sleep from her eyes and shielded them with her hand.

"My place, come on." A lazy smile formed across his mouth and he grabbed her hand, leading her into the one-room log cabin.

Inside, he tossed his car keys and phone on the kitchen table and turned to take her other hand in his, walking backward through the small space toward the armchair in the corner. "Here, you sit here, and I'll make another pot of coffee. We can hash things out. You can stay as long as you need to. Your family is welcome to come here after they are released, too." His offer was genuine but she shook her head, her mouth set in a line.

"Keegan, you don't understand."

He cocked his head and furrowed his brows. "I thought you didn't want to go back to the lodge?"

"No, not that. You're right . . . I don't." A sheepish grin curled the corners of her mouth and a slight flush crept up her cheeks. Her eyes darted around him and she continued. "I mean I *really* need to grab a shower. Would you . . . mind?"

As she said it, she bit down on her lower lip. Keegan's stomach tightened into a knot. Gravely, he nodded his head and began to gesture in the general vicinity of his personal shower.

She stood and followed him straight into the bathroom.

They tumbled through the doorway, their bodies glued together at the sink as layers fell off. Keegan reached a hand out to turn on the shower.

Steam collected on the mirror above his sink before she finally let go of him. He swallowed hard as she brushed aside his flannel shower curtain and gingerly stepped into the hot fog billowing out from the spray of water.

Here they were, reunited after nearly two decades. Alone. Utterly alone. In his bathroom. Half-dressed. And all he could think about was a dead tourist.

CHAPTER 18

Bo peeked out from behind his shower curtain just as he was preparing to follow her in.

But a moment of hesitation crossed his face, and she saw it. She felt it, too.

They locked eyes and she shook her head. "I can't."

He didn't argue, leaving her with a sweet peck on the cheek and returning only to set a fresh towel and clean outfit on the vanity.

After the shower, Bo dried off and studied her reflection through the dewy mirror.

She patted her body dry, slinging the towel evenly over its rack before pulling on Keegan's gray sweatpants and a worn Search and Rescue T-shirt.

Bo strolled out of the bathroom, admiring Keegan's tidy little home. The log walls were bare, showing off the craftsmanship of the cabin. He had no television set or computer, at least that she could see. Simply his bed, two nightstands that held two matching lamps and an array of family photographs, one narrow wardrobe, the armchair and ottoman, and his kitchen table and chairs. Appliances and equipment crowded the otherwise clean kitchen. Exposed cabinetry gave her a view of a modest set of enamelware, a few mixing bowls, and a hodgepodge collection of drinking glasses and mugs.

Keegan was nowhere to be seen, but he'd folded Bo's outfit and set it on the ottoman. She lifted the denim pants and pulled her phone from the back pocket. Exhaustion hit her all over again as she fell into the chair and curled up, swiping her phone awake to see five missed texts and seven missed calls.

She rifled through, taking note that her mother was the lone missed caller and all the texts were also from her. She'd somehow caught wind of the events.

Learning more about the case felt impossible under the circumstances. But then, she realized, she could look online. The whole community was probably abuzz with rumors and gossip, at the very least. All she had to do was tap open her social media app and navigate to the paper's page.

But there it was. Right away. The squat preview of a breaking news story sat squarely at the top of her feed. Her mouth set in a line and her nostrils flared as she clicked it open.

POLICE: Tourist's body found in local lake

Paul Zick — Mountain Times *Editor-in-Chief*

Maplewood Police Department has confirmed that the body of an unnamed woman was recovered from Hogtown Lake in the early morning of Thursday, July 5.

Local fisherman Logan Zick, whose property abuts the lake, helped notify police of his grisly discovery. Zick declined to comment, despite his relationship with two staff members of the Mountain Times.

Police Chief Denny Vogel has confirmed that Apache County will work in cooperation with town law enforcement in an exhaustive investigation of the mysterious death. Sources suggest a connection between the victim and Maplewood's own Wood Smoke Lodge.

Check back with the* Mountain Times *for exclusive, late-breaking news on Maplewood's most important story.

"Everything okay?"

Bo looked up to see Keegan filling the doorway. His hands gripped the top of the frame, his lean body stretched up.

She shook her head. "They already ran an article. Paul wrote it himself." Disbelief swirled around her.

"Well, I guess you and I are two peas in a pod," he answered.

Her brows fell and she tossed the phone onto the ottoman before she stood and stretched herself. "What do you mean?"

"Mandatory leave. Just got off the phone with the county chief." He pulled a hand back and thwacked the wall space above the door before falling inside and slamming it behind him. "He confirmed my sentence."

Bo swallowed. This was all her fault. Keegan did nothing but help her, and she repaid him with a sleepless night in an Adirondack chair and a very clear connection to a very dead tourist. Here they were, both suspended from work and both at risk of being arrested.

"What the hell, though? I mean, what about Michael? They booked him, right?" She was sleep-starved and her head throbbed. She pressed her fingers to either side of her temples, working the pain away from her eyes.

Keegan stalked to his bed and fell back onto it, anchoring his hands behind his head. "Hate to tell you this, Bo, but it's not looking good. He could just as easily tell the cops we were the last to see her. It's our word against his."

Bo felt dizzy. *No, no, no.* "No freakin' way. Keegan, there's no way, right? We can't be real suspects. They'd have brought us back in. Right?"

He shook his head, a frown pulling at his mouth. She began to pace, new energy buzzing through her as though a fly had crawled under her skin and was trying desperately to get out. She wasn't going down for the murder of some whorish stalker who lived in the *Valley*. She thought about what would happen next. She'd have to hire a lawyer. Maybe she and Keegan could share one with Mary and Kurt?

What the hell was going on at the station? Why hadn't she heard anything? Should she call her brothers? What was the right thing to do?

"Keegan." She halted in her tracks, facing the bed, hands on her hips. "Keegan, listen to me, okay?"

He mumbled something before rubbing his face.

"Keegan, I'm not going to become a victim here. So that leaves us with one option: we have to solve the case."

CHAPTER 19

Keegan rolled up to a sitting position, raking his hands through his hair and staring into Bo's watery, crystalline eyes.

"Let's do it."

They got to work. Keegan pulled a notepad from one of his kitchen drawers and a pencil from the cup on the island. At the station, when a case first hit, their planning was structured and procedural. He could apply those principles here, but Bo seemed rabid to take over. Like her life depended on it.

He supposed both their lives did.

He tore off several pages of the notepad and grabbed a second pencil from the cup, and together, they sat at the kitchen table, pencils poised, brows furrowed.

"Where do we start?" She glanced at him, her face serious.

He stood and lifted his chair, swinging it around to her side of the table, where he positioned it backward and straddled it. Hunched over the short chairback and onto the wooden surface, he slapped down his pages and drew a line across the top one. "Timeline. I'll start it. You list everyone we saw last night. Everyone at the party, first. Then a second list: everyone at the bar. Make a list of the names of the people staying at the lodge, too."

Keegan feverishly scribbled onto his page, knocking out his task in minutes. He rose and moved to the counter where he pulled two mugs from the shelf above the sink and splashed fresh coffee into each, returning to the table with them to review what he had as Bo continued to murmur to herself as she categorized her list.

As she stopped to sip her coffee, he cut in. "Okay, here we go. Nine o'clock, we leave the lodge and go to Last Chance. Thirty minutes later, or so, Michael and I see this woman stumble inside. Then about ten . . . Wait!"

He stopped, slamming his cup down on the table, black liquid sloshing onto the waxed oak surface. "Wait a minute, Bo." He drilled a stare into her as she sat there, her eyes wide. "We saw Brittany come into the bar. Michael had eyes on her. As soon as she was inside, he left the deck. I didn't see him again until you brought them both back to the lodge."

Bo lifted her hands to her mouth, her face softening. "Michael went after her then?"

"I don't know, but it's a perfect coincidence, don't you think?"

A light bulb clicked on for her, too, and she nodded her head furiously. "Yes, yes he did! When she came up to me at the bar, she complained about some guy hitting on her! It must have been him. Who else in that bar would hit on a flatlander?"

He bent over the table and scratched out more notes before studying the paper, his eyes bright. "Okay, so Michael sees her and talks her up, but it doesn't pan out. He goes back in. Dutch and I return ten minutes later. Maybe sooner. You and I talk to Kara. I take Kara home. By then, it's probably only ten o'clock. Maybe eleven, if we want to be liberal in our estimate."

Bo blinked up at him. "And then we showed up about half an hour later, right?"

"Well, it felt longer to me. I think I checked the clock at one point. I definitely remember it was before midnight, though."

He scratched his head and made a note. Bo scooted her chair back from the table and draped one leg over the other. "Let's say I arrived at the lodge at eleven. Michael walked Brittany upstairs right away. You and I went outside and . . . "

"Yeah," he answered, a grin pricking one corner of his mouth.

"Okay, what time did we hear the car? How long had we been outside?" She glanced over at his rough timeline. "An hour or so?"

He blew out a sigh and crossed his arms. "Maybe? Yeah. Dang." He dropped back on the chair and picked up the pencil. "Okay, let's say an hour. It's midnight and we think someone comes in. Or was it someone leaving?"

Bo propped her chin in her hand and looked around, her bare face somber and thoughtful. "Don't you remember? Two cars. We thought it was two cars. One with Mary and Kurt and one with Anna and Dutch. But . . ." She flashed her eyes to his.

Keegan cut in. "Two cars arriving? Or one car arriving and leaving? Could it have been later? Did we sleep through the arrival of your sisters?"

Bo shrugged, helpless. "If we did, then Michael was telling the truth. Someone picked her up."

"I wish we knew when your sisters came back." He threw the pencil down and rubbed his eyes.

As if on cue, Bo's phone chimed awake. She grabbed it, nearly knocking it off the table and onto the floor before squeezing it in both hands and holding it up to her face. Without prompting, she confirmed that it was Mary and looked up at him before returning her gaze to the phone and reading aloud from the glowing screen. *"Just left the station. Kurt and Michael are being held."*

CHAPTER 20

Bo held her breath as they scrambled through the door of Keegan's cabin and peeled out of his drive, the truck heaving down the road and onto the highway, weaving between pre-lunch traffic until he swerved onto Ingleheart Lane, home of Dick and Margaret Delaney. Everyone decided it was the logical place to meet.

The lodge was officially a crime scene, despite the absence of any real crime. So, it was off-limits. The other guests who were loitering behind were put up in Maplewood Motel for the night and told to stay put. Mary wasn't allowed to check out the ones who were already planning to leave. Two groups would be transferred, effectively, to the motel. An older man and his wife. And the two pretty girls and their dopey tagalong. Bo pictured the prissy group as they were forced into a shabby room at the motel. It didn't comfort her.

Gravel shot into the tire wells like shotgun spray as maple trees and aspens blurred by. Keegan threw the truck into park, and Bo broke free from her seat and raced up the steps and through an open door, where Mary stood, her face white as a sheet, her hair wild about her head.

"Are you okay?" Bo grabbed her little sister and cradled her in a hug. Sobs fell from her mouth and Bo looked over Mary's shoulder. In the living room, Kara was curled into a ball on the sofa.

Bo's parents huddled together in the kitchen, prepping food. Her mom's face was flushed. Her dad's was drawn. Anna and Dutch sat on the love seat, motionless and silent.

"Why Kurt?" Bo asked in time for Keegan to cross the threshold and join them at the kitchen table.

Kara let out a sob. "My children. My children!" She wailed, flipping to face the back of the couch. Bo ignored her and asked again.

"Mary, why did they keep Kurt?"

Mary shook her head and peeled away from Bo, running through the house and slamming herself into a bedroom.

Anna stood and followed her, leaving Bo to confront Kara.

Bo looked at Dutch. A man she barely knew. "What happened at the station? Tell me everything."

He launched into a comprehensive review of everything he knew, which was limited to his own observations and whatever Mary and Kara had relayed.

Mary, Kurt, Anna, and Dutch had left the bar at 2am. Eyewitnesses confirmed this, as did the lone security camera hanging outside the deck. The foursome stopped at the corner shop at Dutch's insistence that they grab ingredients for Bloody Marys for the next morning. Anna guessed they had left the shop by 2:30 at the latest and thought further video footage and the shopkeeper's testimony would end up confirming. Bo cringed with every legal term. Finally, they had arrived back at the lodge by three, when each couple quietly crept upstairs and to their own rooms. Everyone claimed to have crashed out, hearing nothing and not waking until early the next morning when Keegan came banging on the door, waking and bewildering everyone.

That was apparently enough to release Anna, Dutch, Kara, and Mary from questioning with the warning to stick around. Chills overcame Bo. She'd received the same threat.

"What about Michael and Kara?"

Dutch looked over Bo's shoulder at the convulsing body on the sofa. "Kara choked out a few words, but we can't understand her. She's been like this ever since the station let us go. Cops wouldn't say a word to us, either. Just told us to keep her in town."

Kara's sobs finally died down into sniffles and erratic heaves.

"So why the hell did they keep Kurt?" Keegan cut in.

Footsteps came down the hall and Bo turned to see Mary and Anna rejoining them. Mary's face tear-streaked and splotchy. Anna's arm firmly wrapped around her shoulders as though she was forcing her back out. "Why'd they keep Kurt?" Bo echoed.

"They found a note in your room. They think Kurt wrote it."

———

Anna offered Kara and Mary both a Xanax, which Kara greedily swallowed and Mary rejected.

Mary brought a blanket and draped it over the woman, shushing her and sinking into the sofa with her.

"I know Kurt didn't do it. He didn't even know Brittany was coming up. He blocked her months ago. After she reached out to him. You have to believe me." Her voice was pleading and dramatic. Kara sobbed again.

Bo stepped to the sofa, dropping next to Mary. "We believe you, Mare. We believe Kurt, too. And we're going to get to the bottom of things. I'm going back to the office. We need answers."

She stood from the sofa and stalked through the cabin and out to Keegan's truck. After climbing in, she waited for him in the cab.

Once alone, she tapped open her social media app. Another news article splashed across the top of her feed. This one, however, really was news to Bo.

POLICE: Murder suspects under arrest

Paul Zick — Mountain Times *Editor-in-Chief*

Police Chief Denny Vogel has released an official statement to the press in which he confirms that two summer visitors are being detained for further investigation in the murder of a Phoenix woman.

Neither the chief nor the department spokesperson is releasing the names of the suspects, but the brief statement indicated evidence or highly damning information had been uncovered.

Next-of-kin notifications have begun. As soon as the names have been released to the press, they will be reported here. The victim's body was found by local fisherman Logan Zick early in the morning of July 5. Sources have not revealed if the location of the discovery was also the murder site, but it seems highly doubtful at this time.

Check back with the Mountain Times *for exclusive, late-breaking news on Maplewood's most important story.*

CHAPTER 21

Keegan threw the truck into gear and put his phone on speaker after dialing Carl.

"'Sup, man. Heard about your raw deal. You're clear now, right? They just got the guy, I heard." Carl's voice was low over the phone, and Keegan suspected word was out about his involvement.

"Haven't heard from the chief yet. I'm keeping my space until I get the clear from him. But Carl, I gotta know. What did they find?" He glanced at Bo, who was staring intently at the phone.

He wanted to remind her that Carl was a Search and Rescue officer. He probably knew nothing. The call was a last ditch effort before Bo stormed the paper offices and made a scene. Maybe they could work the case another way.

"Give me a minute, Keegan," Carl whispered before the phone went mute.

Bo's folks lived in the heart of town near the newspaper office. Soon enough, he steered the truck into a space in the gravel lot and shut off the engine. She seemed to consider whether to stay or go inside. Inside, where her boss might have the scoop but might not share it. Here, where Carl might not have the scoop at all but would share it if he did.

He waved a hand, encouraging her to go in. He could fill her in when she returned. She curled a hand around the door handle but paused and locked eyes with him. "If it's true, Keegan," she began. He watched her lips move, wondering if she was thinking the same thing. "Then we're off the hook."

She hopped out of the truck and he kept his eye on her as she scurried inside in his sweats and T-shirt. He liked that she was wearing his clothes. It made them feel impossibly close, despite the fact that they'd only barely reconnected. Despite the fact that a murder investigation had cut like a knife through their delicate, newly formed bond.

As soon as her slight frame slipped into the building, Carl came back on the line.

"Hey, man. Sorry about that. You there?"

Keegan said he was.

"Dude, Keegan, they got an ID on the dead body. Some ASU girl. Robinson. Joanie Robinson."

CHAPTER 22

Once Bo stepped into the office, the rhythmic clicking of keyboards assured her no meeting was in progress. The paper was thin on employees. Just a handful of writer-types covering everything from reporting to editing to distribution. Curious faces glanced up over cubicle walls when Bo entered, but she ignored them and moved toward the lone corner office that belonged to Paul.

Bo stopped in front of the door, which was closed. Bo had never seen Paul's office door closed before. She began to knock, but hushed voices behind the particle board piqued her interest and she dropped her hand. She glanced behind her to see if the others were still watching her, waiting for some scandal to unfold before their eyes. But no. They'd resumed their work, heads down and eyes trained on computer screens.

She stood against the wall as though she were waiting for a scheduled appointment. Keeping her eyes down, she quieted her racing heart so she could hear better.

Two men's voices. One was Paul. The other was

familiar but she couldn't nail it down. Their conversation filtered through the door in fragments. She caught phrases and single words and struggled to put them together.

The voices grew louder, alerting Bo to their movement toward the door where she stood. She stepped a couple feet away and pulled out her dead phone, pretending to scroll as she waited.

The door broke open. "Speak of the devil."

Bob Flanagan. Cheery as a son-of-a-bitch.

Bo glanced behind him to find Paul, who seemed unmoved by her appearance. She lifted her eyebrows at him. He shoved his hands in his pockets. "Hi, Roberta. We were just talking about you." A half-smile broke out on his thin lips while his crepey skin grayed under the yellow fluorescents.

"Oh? All good things, I expect." She couldn't help herself. Bo was unused to Paul acting smarmy, but then again, here he was with his new best friend.

Bob took the liberty of joining the false banter. "Actually, yes. Surely you heard? The architect who was staying at your sister's lodge? He fessed up."

Bo felt her knees buckle and her phone nearly slipped from her hand. Confessed? Michael? The crummy timeline Keegan had scrawled out on paper flashed in her mind.

This meant he had lied to her. Brittany never got a ride to a motel. "To what? Is it Brittany? Is it her body?" she demanded.

Bob and Paul both nodded as though they understood she'd take the news a certain way. This time, Paul answered. "Well, we were just about to call you. Roberta, we want *you* to find out what exactly is going on. You're back on the case."

A broad smile crashed across Paul's crooked teeth and Bo felt sick. "Now? What changed?"

Bob cackled. "I don't want to speak for Paul, but I'd imagine the reason is that you're no longer a murder suspect."

Bo's blood turned cold as a picture continued to form in her mind. Wood Smoke? Murder? Yeah, she wanted suspicion off of her. But did it have to mean someone was killed in her sister's lodge? Her sister's . . . home? Her *own* home? Was that someone . . . Brittany?

All she could do was nod, because beneath the horror and her fear was the one thing Bo had come to survive on: an obsessive curiosity.

Before she dipped back out, Paul stopped her. "Wait, Roberta. Just to clarify one point . . . He didn't confess to murder."

She squinted at him. What the hell?

"He confessed to sleeping with her."

CHAPTER 23

"Did you hear?" Keegan asked as Bo hauled herself inside, breathless and flushed.

"Hear what?"

He deadpanned. "It's not Brittany."

Bo's eyes grew wide and her mouth fell open. "So she's okay? Did she turn up? Whose body is it?" Questions tumbled out of her mouth as she leaned closer to him and tucked a strand of her hair behind her ear.

"Some girl from ASU. I don't know. Tourist. My buddy said the search is underway for Brittany, but now, they are looking into a connection. I'm still off the case. Search and Rescue is doubling their efforts, I'm sure. I wish I could freaking get out there." He stared out the front window.

"Keegan, we're going to handle this. We're going to find out about the dead girl. We're going to find Brittany. Drive."

"Where?"

"I need to see the lodge. It's the logical starting point, especially if Brittany is connected to this dead girl. I'm writing a piece for the paper now. Paul put me back on the case. We have to beat those assholes."

"What assholes?"

"Channel Five, for starters. Probably others. Paul said the story is going global. Your dad was in there, too. He didn't know about the body, though. He was more excited about the fact that Michael admitted to sleeping with Brittany."

A pit formed in Keegan's stomach, but it had little to do with the obvious fact that Michael *would* sleep with a drunken stranger while his wife snoozed in the room next door.

No, that didn't affect him or surprise him.

What bothered him was his dad nosing around in the case.

Bob Flanagan might be Maplewood's honestly elected town servant, but in reality, he was a wannabe politician. *Locals* believed he put local issues first. After all, council meetings ran smoothly. Taxes weren't *too* high. The Maplewood Hogs might win a state championship soon. And so forth. *Tourists* came to town and saw Mr. Small-Town Mayor. Americana. Quaint. Salt of the earth. For out-of-towners, he'd bend over backward. "They drive our economy, Keegan," he'd said over and over again.

Local hero. Mountain mayor.

But when a person is two opposite things, that usually means he is neither of them.

Keegan knew Bo understood his dad. She was maybe one of the few people who did, other than him.

"Is Michael involved in the murder? What else did Paul say? It doesn't add up."

She swiveled in her seat, her eyes flashing. "I know, right? Keegan, don't you think that's nuts? Michael sleeps with her, fine. That makes him a scumbag. Not a killer of some other random girl. And why is Kurt still at the station? If they know the body isn't Brittany, then why aren't they changing course?"

"I don't think they're going to let us into the lodge, Bo," he answered, his voice even.

She shook her head. "We have to try. I want to grab my charger. And I want to see where they are focusing their efforts. If they know something we don't."

He simply drove on. Lost in thought. Thoughts about Bo. Thoughts about Michael, the smarmy architect. Thoughts about Brittany. Thoughts about Kurt. The note. A sudden realization overtook him just as they pulled up to the lodge.

Rubberneckers parked along the highway, gawking solemnly down the lane and past a ribbon of police tape. A single cruiser was stationed horizontally, blocking the narrow road from intruders.

The lodge hung among the pine trees like a ship on a still lake.

Keegan waved to the cop reclining lazily in the driver's seat of the car. The cop waved him in, uncaring.

Before they pulled up to a stop in front of the lodge, Keegan put a hand on Bo. He had to tell her. They had to get in touch with Mary. With the station.

"Bo, the note they found . . ."

"Yeah?" She waited.

"I wrote it."

Bo leaned away, caught off guard. "You left a note for

Brittany?" Her eyes wrinkled at the edges and her mouth fell into a deep frown.

"No, no. It was for you. I was so beat. Today has been crazy. I forgot about it. We have to contact the station and let them know. And your sister, too."

Bo's face softened and her body relaxed. A quiet laugh escaped her lips. "Oh, well, what did it say?"

He grinned like a schoolboy. "I just said I was going to grab coffee and that I'd be right back. I signed it 'K' instead of Keegan."

She smiled. "I'll text Mary. You call the station. Maybe they already figured out that it was irrelevant."

He nodded and considered what *was* relevant in the case. So many missing pieces. "Bo, did Brittany drive herself to the bar?"

"Yeah, remember? You saw her walk from her car, right?" He nodded and she went on. "Keegan, for all we know, Brittany hooked up with Michael and then cruised on down to a motel. She might be sleeping it off still. Her car's still probably at the Last Chance, right?"

They weren't sure. The cops hadn't yet made any announcements. Paul Zick, Editor-in-Chief was useless in finding the scoop. If Brittany was on the run, then she had her car. But if her car was at the Last Chance, then Brittany was still in Maplewood. Somewhere.

CHAPTER 24

Bo left Keegan in the reception with the guard. The two men immediately concerned themselves with calling into the station with news of Keegan's faux pas. She needed to get upstairs. Fortunately, the Maplewood Murder Unit was green enough to let her.

In disposable booties and a paper haircap, she rushed up to her room.

The forensics team had just left. The detectives were at the station. She had enough privacy to grab her charger and a few other things then scan her room carefully. Fingerprints had been dusted for. Her bed had been stripped barer than before. Drawers were left open. Her wardrobe agape, hangers haphazardly replaced.

Had her phone been charged, she'd have snapped some shots. Instead, she took her last few moments to walk past Michael's room, the door of which was yawning open. She'd given the detectives her house key, but Michael still had her room key. She saw now that they'd forced entry into his room. Reckless. Unnecessary. Bo thought of Mary, who would have to pay for this damage, no doubt. She'd find a way to help her little sister.

At the bottom of the staircase, Keegan was chatting with the cop and hopefully finished with absolving poor Kurt of any implication. She stole the opportunity to tiptoe all the way into Michael and Kara's guest room.

It had been similarly worked. Bare bed. But fewer items remained. In fact, none remained. All the luggage must have been bagged and tagged. All personal effects.

Sweeping her eyes once more over the room, something caught her eye on the dresser. It was the Wood Smoke welcome packet.

On a whim, Bo grabbed the packet and slipped it into the back of her sweats just before hearing footsteps down below. She quickly dipped out of the room and down the hall, descending the staircase carefully in her booties, joining the two men at the side table near the great room.

"Thank you so much." She offered her hand to the cop, who awkwardly accepted, shaking her hand limply. At the last minute, she asked, "Can I just grab my purse from the reception desk?"

He waved a hand that way and returned his attention to Keegan, who threw a surreptitious glance at Bo but said nothing.

Thank God for crappy cops who couldn't follow procedure if their lives depended on it.

She walked up to the reception and plucked a brochure out of each slot before grabbing one of Mary's Wood Smoke packets and shoving it all into her purse, which was indeed sitting under the register as always.

————

Bo pulled the packet from the back of her sweats as Keegan turned out of the lodge and onto the highway.

"What'd you take?" Exasperation crept into his voice, and Bo steeled herself for a reprimand. He was in law enforcement. How far would he let her go with a rogue investigation? She was about to find out.

Instead of removing the packets and brochures from her satchel, she buckled it closed and leaned back. "Mary puts together a little registration packet for guests. It's hokey, but it includes a pamphlet or flyer from any Maplewood locale that offers one."

"Yeah, I saw. That's where I wrote you a note."

She couldn't help but smile. She wondered why they'd keep Kurt based on a note with the letter K. It probably had more to do with his relationship with Brittany, and less to do with a stupid brochure. "So, when I went into Michael's room upstairs, I saw one of her welcome packets. Maybe the cops overlooked it? Or maybe they grabbed the one from our room and didn't think about picking up Michael's, too?"

Keegan looked at her. "You shouldn't have gone in there." A grin pricked the corners of his mouth.

She didn't agree. Investigative journalism demanded courage. Courage would take them to the killer.

But first, they had to go to the lake. It may not have been the crime scene, but it was an important piece of the puzzle.

They made it to Hogtown Lake Road within minutes.

Keegan slowed his truck before turning. "What about Old Man Zick? Is he going to let us walk around? And cops? Bo, keep your hopes in check. We probably won't be able to get out and walk around."

Her stomach cramped. Even if there was no roadblock or police tape, Logan Zick may not let them walk the property. He acted like he owned it.

Bo thought for a minute. *Did he?*

"Keegan, does Logan *own* the lake?"

He scratched his jaw and Bo noticed a shadow had cascaded across his lower face. Butterflies swirled in her stomach and she forced them down so she could focus. She had to get a sense of the lake. She had no idea how Joanie was killed. Maybe she wasn't drowned. Maybe something else happened first.

"I don't think he owns it personally, but back when the area was first settled, the Zicks laid claim to all of Hogtown. Hell, it was named for their pig farm, actually. Then the original Zicks got stingy with land and new lakes were discovered out west. After the other settlers gave up on negotiating with the Zicks, they established Maplewood. Hogtown became nothing more than a ghost settlement."

A chill coursed through Bo. She'd heard the lore herself, but she never knew where the line lay between fact and fiction. No one knew what happened so many years ago between the Zicks and all those who came to the mountain *after* the Zicks.

Keegan pressed the accelerator and they soon found out that Logan Zick would be the least of their problems.

An entire news crew had set up camp on a shoulder of the dirt road across from Logan's cabin and adjacent to the lake. A camper trailer leaned into the pines, and outside of that stood a small group of people. In front of them, a sturdy tripod supported an oversized video camera. Cords and cables slithered from the legs of the tripod under a mat and into the camper.

Nearer to the lake, various police cruisers and Search and Rescue SUVs lined the road, blocking the news van from access.

Bo glanced toward Logan's house, astounded this could be happening in such close proximity to the old hermit. "How can they be here?"

Keegan eased off the gas and pulled up to a stop about twenty-five yards from the crew. "I don't know."

"Press can't just hang out at an open investigation." But she knew they could come pretty dang close.

He agreed and she told him to stay put while she found out what was up. He noted he would keep an eye on Zick's windows, just in case a shotgun happened to be propped opposite the camera tripod.

Before she pushed out of the truck, Bo commented, "He probably isn't here. He can't just live next door while all this goes on."

Bo approached the group, who'd been watching her since she descended from Keegan's truck. One woman, dressed professionally and wielding a microphone, stepped out and opened a hand to Bo. "Heather Coleman, Channel Five News out of the Valley." Her script was pristine. Cutting. Off-putting.

"Bo Delaney, *Mountain Times* out of Maplewood." Bo

was well aware of the fact that she looked every bit the part of a low-budget local in her oversized County Search and Rescue tee and billowing men's sweats. She didn't care. She could match wit for wit with anyone. When she wanted to.

And today, she wanted to.

CHAPTER 25

As soon as Bo arrived at the reporter huddle, Keegan spotted movement in Zick's cabin. A threadbare flannel window curtain swung next to the door. Moments later, Zick himself busted onto the rotted, sagging porch.

No gun, thankfully.

Instead, the old man screamed. Keegan had never heard an old man scream before. Not at baseball games after a bad call. Not from his own father when a council vote didn't go his way. Not ever.

"No more! Get the hell out of here, the lot of ya!"

Keegan pushed his door open and strode the fifty yards across the road and over to Logan's drive. He kept his hands up and an even expression on his face. "Mr. Zick? I'm Sheriff Keegan Flanagan. Calm down, sir. Please."

"Flanagan? One of Bob's boys?" Zick scratched his hand across a yellow-stained wife beater. His eyes were bleary and a few hairs sat matted atop his head.

Keegan flicked his eyes toward the cops roaming the

scene. They began to take notice of the altercation and started striding over.

"We saw each other this morning, Mr. Zick. I was here with Bo." Keegan pointed toward her as she and the group watched on.

"I remember. I didn't know you were the son-of-a-bitch. Or son-of-an-asshole. Both apply, I 'spose." A lazy grin drew across the man's snaggletoothed mouth before he coughed up a wad of phlegm. Keegan braced himself for Zick to hock it at him. Instead, he swallowed it down in a gulp and wiped the back of his hand across his mouth, clearing away leftover spittle. "Get the hell out of here, Flanagan. And take that damn news van with you before I use it as target practice." Keegan looked back at the group and saw Bo and an overdressed woman break away and move toward him and Zick.

"It's not up to me, Logan. They're free to be here same as Bo and me. Same as you. Lake's public property."

"My ass it's public property. This is Zick land and you know it. That Delaney bitch knows it. Her sisters sure as hell do."

Keegan lifted his eyes as Bo approached, the over-dressed woman at her heels. "It doesn't matter what I know or what my sisters know. This is an active crime scene. So, Logan, how come *you* are allowed to be here?"

CHAPTER 26

The question was important, and Bo just handed it on a silver platter to some bimbo broadcaster.

It also forced the cops to shoo everyone away, including Logan. Though Bo wasn't sure if he simply returned to his house or if the cops forced him to go elsewhere for the night.

They were back in the truck and Bo was moaning about the news team.

It killed her to let that woman scoop them. But then again, Bo *was* the scoop. And she wasn't talking. She was writing. And she had an in that Heather-Coleman-with-Channel-Five didn't: Keegan and his deep network of buddy cops.

He dialed a number now, speaking in a low voice to an unnamed person on the other end. He'd told her he could dig around, but he wasn't giving her source names (obviously) and she couldn't quote him as a source, either (fine).

All she heard was Keegan's side of the conversation.

Yesses. Nos. Ahas. Mmms. And, finally, "Thanks again, man."

He turned to her, his eyes blazing with fire. "We're not going to the station, but I got info. Do you want to go back to your folks' house with the others or . . . ?"

She knew the only other option.

She weighed the two sides. At her folks' house, she had access to Kara. Kara, who—by now—was no doubt privy to her husband's dirty exploits. Kara, who might be willing to shed light on the events of the night before. Kara, who might be as nutty sober as she was drunk.

If Bo went to Keegan's house, she had access to *Keegan*. Keegan, who was about to give her insider info. Keegan, who was a law enforcement officer. Keegan, who would drive her anywhere she wanted. Keegan, who, since high school, had been driving her wild.

"Your place."

He brought her up to speed during the short ride over.

Michael Erinhard had confessed only to sleeping with Brittany. But he denied foul play, instead sticking to his story about Brittany calling a driver. His lawyer was en route from Phoenix, though he may have already arrived in town. Keegan's source was uncertain.

Evidence was desperately lacking.

The note Keegan had copped to was immediately set aside and Kurt had been released. Thank God.

Michael could still be lying. That was obvious to Keegan. But they weren't sure the extent of the lie.

Keegan's pal told him the autopsy was underway and the cops were chasing leads on the car service and the motel. No one had confirmation as to whether Brittany even made it to a car or to a motel. All they knew was she screwed Michael then fell off the radar. No phone pings. No card hits. And, she did not return to her *own* car, which had been collected from the Last Chance and taken to a warehouse for a work-up. That was it. Her parents were coughing up REWARD-IF-FOUND promises on the news in Phoenix and were due to arrive on the mountain themselves.

Just great.

Bo stomped her leg in the cab and let out a curse.

"Oh, and by the way, does Kara know?" she asked once they were inside his place. She fell into his armchair, exhaustion pulling at the back of her eyes. Her nagging headache returned as she realized it was well past lunch and nearly suppertime.

"She knows he's a cheater. Told me so in the car last night."

"Told you what?" Bo's eyes shot up toward Keegan.

"Told me he was cheating on her."

"How come you're just now admitting this?" Bo fumed. She thought they were working this together. He had every chance to say something.

He shook his head and rubbed his eyes. "Bo, we haven't stopped. And what does it matter? It's no surprise the guy's a doucher."

"Keegan, what the hell?" She sighed and sank deeper into the chair.

"Sorry, Bo. Does it change anything? Do you really think Michael is innocent just because he said so? What could Kara have to do with it?"

She leaned forward again and rested her head in her

hands. "We are missing major pieces to the case. We don't even know how or where Joanie died. We don't even know who she is." Something tugged on her memory. A familiarity in the name. She couldn't put a finger on it and went back to her diatribe. "And what about Kara? How come they didn't hold her for questioning? Are they bringing her in?"

"Maybe." He tossed his phone on his bed and pulled his shirt over his head. Bo's stomach fluttered to life. She swallowed a lump and looked away into the kitchen.

She watched as he moved into the bathroom, where he turned on the faucet, turned it off, whipped a towel off the rack, and came back out, drying his face and bringing a clean, fresh smell with him. Again, she averted her eyes.

He crossed in front of her and went into the kitchen, where he turned the oven on and extracted a frozen pizza from the freezer before cracking open two beers and handing one to her.

"Once we know if Brittany made it anywhere after the lodge, then we'll know if Michael's clear. Kara, too, for that matter." She took a swig and tucked a strand of hair behind her ear, following the rippling muscles in Keegan's back as he worked on pulling out two plates and setting them at the table.

He turned around in time to catch her watching him.

She bit her lip and rose from the chair, her loins throbbing.

His phone rang, startling her. It didn't chime. It didn't beep. It didn't vibrate. It rang.

Her eyes danced around his pants, looking for his cell. But he didn't reach for a cell phone. Instead, he turned on a heel and paced back into the kitchen, where he picked up a previously unseen landline. Cord and all.

"Hello?"

Bo sank back into the chair and let out a breath as she watched him.

"Hey, hey, hey, slow down. Where? Who?" His eyes shot up to meet Bo's. "Thanks, gotta go."

"What?" Bo stood, searching him. Frantic to know.

He dropped the receiver back onto its cradle and swallowed before meeting her gaze. "The body they found. She was one of Mary's guests."

CHAPTER 27

POLICE: One body, three missing persons, zero suspects

Bo Delaney — Mountain Times Reporter

A spokesperson for the Maplewood PD has confirmed the identity of the body discovered in Hogtown Lake.

Joan "Joanie" Robinson, 22, was last seen alive by Mary Delaney at Maplewood's own Wood Smoke Lodge.

Search efforts remain focused on Brittany Purcell-Cutler, a Maplewood visitor who is, by all accounts, unconnected to Robinson. New search efforts are underway for Robinson's travel companions, 21-year-old Kathryn "Kat" Donahue and 21-year-old David Matusewski.

Locals and tourists alike are encouraged to come forward with any information about these cases.

"I can't do it." Bo slammed her laptop shut and shoved it back into her satchel on Keegan's bed. "People are going to think I'm writing a cover-up story for my sister!"

Keegan sank down next to her and reached a hand to her face, sliding an errant strand of hair from her eyes. "Let me take you back to your parents' house. You don't have to cover the case. This is out of our hands, Bo."

They'd swung by the Delaney homestead earlier, after leaving the crime scene. No one had heard the news yet. Mary was distraught. Kurt was freaked out. Bo ignored them both. She just wanted answers. She had no patience to console her sister and the fiancé with an increasingly checkered past.

Dutch and Anna were leaving the mountain first thing Saturday morning, which watered down the melodrama.

Kara was in custody by then, no doubt stalling until Michael's lawyer joined them. Bo fully expected both of the Erinhards to file suit against Maplewood after this mess. She couldn't believe the local law enforcement could be so dense as to think Michael was stupid enough to kill a hook-up. And Kara? She was too odd to be involved. And, anyway, what did they have to do with the three college kids? Squat diddly.

Bo explained to her parents that she was writing about the case. They were appalled. She was practically a victim herself. Why should she have to face all the horror?

Clearly, her parents didn't understand her.

They'd encouraged her to stay the night at the house with Mary and Kurt. But she had different plans. She couldn't be around them. Guilt and fear nagged at her. But more than that, she knew they wouldn't let her get down to business.

And, anyway, Keegan was her partner now.

She had to stay the night with him. They had to work

it. If not for her writing assignment, then at least for justice.

They slept in his bed, but Keegan was on his best behavior. As was Bo. Anyway, they were too tired for any funny business. But even under the weight of exhaustion, Bo tossed and turned, wondering why she was so compelled to put herself in difficult situations. In the past, those situations had never been to anyone's real benefit. She'd been lazy. Rootless. Non-committal.

Now, here she was, back in Maplewood—a place she'd kissed goodbye after high school—and she was caught up in the craziest criminal investigation the tiny town had ever seen.

She had been a suspect, for God's sake. Everyone she knew was a suspect.

Why hadn't the police nailed down specifics? And if they had, then how come no formal statement came out? People were worried. The little mountain hamlet was no longer a safe place to live. *Or* visit.

Around four a.m., Bo gave up on sleep and instead searched the Net. Looking for history on Maplewood's homicide unit was like trying to find D.B. Cooper.

She did learn that the last time someone died under suspicious circumstances was 1997, after a lonely single woman found herself drunk in the middle of the highway. Her death was ruled an accident.

Then, in 2000, a group of tourists from Utah had gone missing, never to be seen or heard from again. Maplewood passed it off to the FBI, who let it go cold by 2005.

Prior to that, there had been a bar fight. 1960s. Two

locals got into it over a girl. One beat the other to death. Manslaughter.

Even further back, Bo stumbled across coverage of Maplewood's only recorded murder. The report was published recently, in 2001, by a now-retired reporter of the name Gloria Fiorillo. In her report, Gloria related the story of Carlton Zick and Aloysius Ingleheart.

Bo's breath caught against Keegan's pillow as she saw the name.

Aloysius Ingleheart was her great uncle and the same man who helped build the cabin in which her parents lived. The one in which she had grown up. Grandpa Garold was Aloysius's nephew and Margaret Delaney's father. Alan was named for Aloysius, who went by Al.

She knew that Al had died young. He wasn't married. Had no kids. But he and his brother George were some of the earliest settlers of Maplewood. But . . . murdered?

Bo read through the article like her life depended on it.

Zick and Ingleheart had gone rounds about whether to stay and settle the Hogtown area or expand the settlement northeast. Zick felt passionate about staying put but was unwilling to parcel out his land, which he'd staked claim to before the Inglehearts had ever arrived.

Al gave up trying to work with Zick and convinced his brood to uproot and find different territory. When other parties followed suit and left the Zicks to fend for themselves against the blizzard of 1904, blood turned bad.

Weeks later, when the mountain thawed, Al Ingleheart was found hacked to death in his barn. The bloodied murder weapon left carelessly in a nearby hay pile? A pig butcher's ax.

Ingelhearts took to the dirt road to avenge their cousin's death, but by the time they'd made it to Hogtown, as the Zicks had named the area, Carlton had already been killed by his own. A lukewarm truce took shape as Zicks gave up their unhallowed territory to assimilate into Maplewood, but Carlton's direct descendants stayed on, farming pigs and fishing as a means for survival and a show of loyalty to their forefather.

Bo clicked out of the article and went to the bathroom, where she splashed water on her face and stared into the dark mirror. Though the night was cool, blood ran hot in her veins.

All her life, she'd let her family down. Getting in trouble as an adolescent. Borrowing money to scrape together a college degree, only to drop out and re-enroll sporadically until she finally made it by the skin of her teeth and through a hush-hush agreement with an amoral dean. She'd let her anxieties get in the way of any real ambition. With each bad choice, she'd punished herself, which only doubled her setbacks.

In high school, after the first time she stole a pack of gum, her parents disciplined her by grounding her to her bedroom for a month and tripling her workload on the farm. All that alone time in her bedroom resulted in lots of nail-picking and nail-biting, which resulted in a skin infection, which resulted in a trip to the hospital for antibiotics, which resulted in a shifting of her duties from farm work to housework. The answer was cleaning. It always was.

Then, the second time she got in trouble (driving drunk, but only barely), her parents sent her to live with her Aunt Irma. There was nothing to do at Aunt Irma's house. Not technically. The place was a mess, though. So the first week, Bo cleaned. When the house was clean, she asked for something else to do. Aunt Irma scuttled over to an ancient typewriter and showed Bo how to use it.

At first, Bo just played with the clunky machine, typing random letters. But then she noticed the thick layer of dust that settled between the keys. After she'd cleaned it, Bo realized she may as well write something. Fifty pages later, she had a story. When Bo returned home with unchewed nail beds and her first-ever story, her parents didn't much care. Life was crazy busy at the farm. Six kids. Countless animals. Crops. And, while Bo was gone, the dishes piled up.

Once Bo was out of the house, she needed a break and opted to skulk in dingy bars throughout the southwest as she cobbled together an independent existent. *Further* irritating her parents. At least she kept her various apartments clean.

Now, she was back on the mountain, and she'd driven a nutcase to her sister's lodge. Could Wood Smoke recover after this?

She'd make sure of it. And the only way to avenge the Wood Smoke victims was to find their killer.

But it wasn't just her sister's business that Bo cared about. It wasn't just the dead flatlanders.

Nope.

Roberta Delaney had a chance to make something of herself. Forge a real career. A vocation, even. A job she cared about. Maybe a passion.

And, not least of all, she had someone to impress.

CHAPER 28

Keegan didn't sleep. Between nightmares and the glow of Bo's phone in bed beside him, it was useless. When he gave up around five a.m., all Keegan could think about was his mother's wild voice on the other end of the line. Her excitement.

So, when he rolled out of bed and grabbed his phone, he was unsurprised to see her text. Unsurprised but disappointed.

His eyes flashed along her accusatory words.

Are you with Roberta? Is she really writing a story about the murders?

He wasn't totally sure where she was going with that line of questioning. But he had an idea.

Bo was in the bathroom, which left him to wander out onto his deck. Fresh dew lifted from the oak saplings and clovers. He dialed his mom.

"Yes. Bo is writing a story, Mom. Why do you ask?"

"Good morning to you, too, Mr. Cranky." Victoria Flanagan was nothing if not falsely cheerful. So, her chipper voice shouldn't have unsettled him. "I'm only asking because it seems the two of you are gettin' a little familiar."

"What are you talking about?"

"Your dad just happened to notice. He says you two are glued to each other. And he's seen Bo around the paper. He knows about her newest assignment. I think it's a fabulous idea!"

He blew out a sigh and rubbed his face with his hand. "Yeah, well. She's trying. Not sure what good it'll do. This whole case is crazy."

"I know, Keegan. Maplewood has made national cable shows. Did you see? We're in every newspaper in America. Every television channel in America! Internationally, too! I wonder how it'll affect the Labor Day Parade." Her voice turned to a low purr.

Keegan checked back through the window to see if he could spot Bo. No such luck.

"Mom, don't worry. By then, it'll have blown over. People will come back to the mountain. They always do."

"Oh, baby, I know. I think this whole thing might even create a bit of a boon. Morbid, I know. But I mean, we're a rural community and every tourist dollar counts, you know, Keegan. Especially in the second-home real estate industry up here."

Keegan scoffed. Second-home real estate industry? Was his mom *this* vapid? Did she care about Mary's lodge? Did she care about the victims or that a murderer was on the loose?

Then it hit him. A horrid revelation. Sickening, really.

If there was one thing in this town that Victoria Flanagan cared about, it was tourism.

———

He hung up on the madwoman and returned through the door.

Bo ducked out from behind the open fridge.

"Sorry, did I wake you?"

He did a double take. She'd changed out of his sweats and into a pair of his boxers and a fresh T-shirt. Her hair was piled in a high mess on her head, tendrils falling about her naked face. She looked gorgeous. He wished he could sweep the horror under a blanket of pine needles and scoop her off back into his bed for a second attempt.

"No," he answered, smiling widely.

She returned the grin and lifted a half gallon of milk up. "Coffee and cream?"

They sipped together at the table, and Bo hurriedly shuffled through her game plan, which was half to-do list and half hard-boiled questions. The questions were mainly Keegan's tasks.

1. Call the list of rideshares she'd found in an online marketplace. "Randos offering shuttle service for drunk flatlanders," she explained.

2. Extensive social media search on the three tourists. Same for Brittany. Same for Kurt. Same for Kara. Notes should be taken.

3. Find out about the autopsy. How did Joanie die? Where?

After number three, she took a breath and lifted her

head. "Four people, Keegan. We have to solve a puzzle involving four people. Do we assume the other three are dead, too?"

He rubbed a hand over his face. "Bo, we don't have any information. And if we did, then what? You'll write a report and publish it in the paper?"

Bo's pocket vibrated and she stretched back to check it.

Paul.

She held the buzzing phone for Keegan to see it before she tapped ANSWER then SPEAKER. "Hey, Paul."

"Roberta, how's your piece coming? We need to get it out ahead of Channel Five. Heather Coleman, specifically. I heard you met her, right? So I suppose you already know she's in town."

Keegan cocked his head and glared at her meaningfully.

She waved him away and carried the phone over to the chair, where she'd left her laptop the night before. "Sending now, Paul." She opened her computer and navigated quickly.

Paul came back on. "Got it. Hang on. Let me read."

Keegan mouthed to her, *How does he know you met her?"* Again, she waved him off, turning away to reread the article she'd given up on the night before.

"Um, Roberta, what the hell? This reads like a report. Where's the grit? Where's the familiarity? I told you *not* to treat your approach as an investigative piece. I gave you the assignment as a human interest narrative. A *personal* human interest narrative. You're not trying to solve the case. I don't want that. You've got twenty minutes to resend or I'm taking it back and writing it myself."

He clicked off and Bo muttered something under her breath before attacking her keyboard. Tears threatened to spill onto the keys, but she didn't want to waste a chance. She'd buck up and do the job her boss was telling her to do. For once, she'd follow directions.

"Wait a sec," Keegan interrupted. She glanced up. "Why did Paul show up at the lake yesterday morning?"

CHAPTER 29

Bo thought for a moment before shrugging. "They're brothers, right? Maybe he was showing up to support Logan?"

Keegan shook his head. "Maybe. Let's pull up a list of rideshares. Craigslist? Facebook? Where do we start?"

She got busy scrolling and jotting down numbers for him to dial. With each answered call came an automatic response. *We already talked to police.*

None of the drivers who spoke with Keegan admitted to driving a Brittany Cutler or any other drunk blonde anywhere, and especially not after midnight. At least one of the drivers could have been lying, of course. But why would they lie? What reason would a random person have to dispose of a tourist? None.

With the driver search exhausted, Keegan chucked his phone on the table. "Michael's lying."

Bo nodded in solemn agreement as she downed the rest of her mug. The coffee maker beeped a warning cry. It was about to shut itself off. Keegan rose from his seat and stabbed it back on, refilling his and her mugs and leaving the carafe on the hot pad.

"Do we assume it's him as we move forward? Or do we keep our minds open? How do you think the cops are handling the same info?"

She hadn't done many investigative reports in her time. *Or* personal narratives, for that matter. Mostly just fluff pieces on dogs in pajamas and cats who walked on leashes. Oh, yeah. And Sonoran hot dogs. Bo felt utterly inept when it came to a *murder* report. And though Paul wanted her to write something weird and flowery and fictionalized, she was still treating her project as a murder report. Because who the hell would care about *her* in all this? Paul's focus was odd and off-kilter.

She would have to ignore him. For the sake of the paper. *His* paper.

"Cops are going to consider that they can't trace a driver. No doubt. What we really need to know are the autopsy results. What happened to Joanie? How was she killed? Where was she killed? Why the lake? And when did Michael come across Joanie? Are her friends dead, too? Is Michael a serial killer on the loose? I highly doubt it."

He was on a roll, but she interrupted. "And how did the killer know where the lake was? Does Michael know about Hogtown? It's nearby but tucked away. More of a local attraction than a tourist one."

She hated to admit it, but it was true. Could a Maplewood local be to blame? Bo couldn't stomach the thought. Sure, there were many nutjobs who lived and worked in Maplewood year-round. But they were *her* people. It was *her* town. *Her* mountain. The thought solidified something in Bo she hadn't yet come to terms with: for the past decade or more, she hadn't been rootless. Or noncommittal. Or flaky. She had been *homesick*.

"Exactly." He pulled a fresh page onto the table and sat to jot down the questions. As his handwriting took form on the page, a bulb went on in her head.

"Wait!"

She scrambled from the table and to her satchel, where she dug for a moment before pulling out Mary's brochures and the one she'd found in Michael and Kara's guest room. "Ah-ha!"

She began with one of the unused packets, which would match exactly what Michael (and, therefore, Brittany) would have had access to before the night went on.

The brochure included almost every public location in Maplewood. Advertisers needn't have paid for a spot. Nearly all local businesses were covered in the description of the town. Keegan looked over Bo's shoulder, and together, they read through the tri-folded cardstock.

Welcome to Wood Smoke Lodge on Arizona's own Maplewood Mountain!

Here you'll find info on just about every spot in town, complete with directions and phone numbers. Just remember, there's no rush to see it all. You can extend your stay at the lodge if you want. After all, up here, we're on MOUNTAIN TIME!

DAYBREAK:

Enjoy a hearty brunch at Darci's Hometown Cafe! Maplewood Blvd. East of Mountain Gas 'N Go and west of the firehouse.

NOON:

Pack a lunch and have a picnic kayak ride on Maplewood Lake just off the Boulevard and behind Darci's! Pick up your vessel at Mountain Sports on the corner of Hogtown Rd. and Maplewood Blvd.

QUITTIN' TIME:

Dinner and drinks at Jimmy Jake's Steaks. Southeast corner of Maplewood Hwy. and Maplewood Blvd.

FUN IN THE SUN:

Don't forget to head up to the ski slopes for summer activities such as daily BBQs and evening ski lift rides.

OR: Hit one of our many local lakes for a quick fishing trip (SEE MAP ON REVERSE).

SHOPAHOLICS:

Big Ed's Market is a one-stop shopping experience. Swing in for everything from a pair of wool socks to a cup of fishin' worms. You might even run into Big Ed himself!

Keegan picked the paper out of her hand and flipped it over to where the map was drawn.

Her eyes ran the along the back of the narrow page, searching for something—anything—to point them in the right direction.

Funny things were labeled. It was a confusing reference guide, including an arrow to a Laundromat and a heart encompassing Darci's Café. But then trailheads and lakes were indicated in the usual way in which a cartographer might design a map.

But Mary's map was a mess of information. Practically useless to anyone who didn't know the area.

Keegan tossed the brochure onto the table just as his phone rang from the kitchen counter. He strode to it and answered, keeping his eyes on her. "Hello?"

Moments passed and he hung up with little more than a *thanks*. "Let's go. Bring your computer."

"Why?"

"It was my dad." A sigh escaped his mouth as he reached for his keys.

Rising from the table, she tucked her phone in her pocket and jogged to her satchel, stuffing in the brochure and double-checking her computer was safe inside. "Where are we going?" she pressed.

"Channel Five is requesting a press conference at the town center. My dad says we're about to be scooped."

CHAPTER 30

They pulled up to the grassy knoll that sprawled between St. Magdalene's and St. Patrick's. Once Bo climbed out of the truck, Keegan followed her to the small crowd forming on the green. He had no idea what his dad meant or how the Phoenix broadcaster had gotten insider information. But they were about to find out.

He spotted his parents behind two microphones. Next to Bob stood Chief Vogel and two other uniforms—Dawson and Biggans. Paul Zick crossed his arms over his chest behind Victoria.

The woman with the news station was there, too. Clad in a fresh red blazer, her cadre of useless extras fanned out behind her, wires tangled around them. One studied her through the bulky camera.

Onlookers drifted into the growing crowd, though Keegan wasn't sure how they knew about the conference or where they came from.

A hipster type directed from his position behind a rolling camera as Heather Coleman adjusted her helmet head and ran her tongue across her expansive white teeth as she stood to the left of the hulking recorder.

Keegan lifted his eyebrows as the impromptu event unfolded in a flash. His dad cleared his throat and flashed a broad grin to the people who'd stopped milling about and shushed each other to hear him.

The man with the thick-framed glasses became agitated and waved his hand frantically to move Heather into the frame. Bob Flanagan tapped the microphone.

"Is this thing on?" To Keegan's great shock, the easy, down-home, small-town veneer cracked when no one laughed with Bob as he fumbled in raising the microphone to meet his clean-shaven face. He cleared his throat a second time.

"For those tuning in, I'm Mayor Flanagan, in case you don't know," he began, glancing to Victoria, who offered a not-so-subtle thumbs up. "By now, you might have heard that the body of a deceased Phoenix woman was found up at Hogtown Lake yesterday morning." No response from the crowd. Bob shifted his weight and looked the other way toward Paul, who nodded solemnly and peered out at the crowd. He uncrossed his arms and tucked his hands into his pants pockets.

Bob went on. "You might also have heard about the three other tourists who are now labeled missing persons." From the cacophony of gasps, it was clear the crowd was far less aware of the latest development. Keegan looked at Bo, who flicked a glance up to him. A brief smile thinned her lips and she reached for his hand. He took it, lacing his fingers into hers.

The crowd fell silent and allowed Bob to continue. He

earned some confidence from breaking the news. His body relaxed and his hands opened. "Maplewood's Chief of Police, Denny Vogel, is joining us today to share information that may assist authorities in solving the open investigation." His eyes narrowed on Keegan, but his expression was unreadable. Bo squeezed his hand.

Vogel stepped up to the microphone and thanked Bob quietly before launching into his overview.

They'd left the conference before the hordes of people descended on them. After all, quite a many in the crowd knew Bo. And they knew she was Mary's sister. And they knew Mary owned Wood Smoke.

A short drive later, the two rolled into the back parking lot of the police station, where Carl had told Keegan to meet him. They parked behind the dumpster and sat in the truck, unsure what to say to each other.

Finally, Bo broke the silence. "Why did your dad want us there? There was no scoop. No new info. Even Heather-Coleman-with-Channel-Five was irritated."

Keegan shook his head. "I bet the chief didn't even want a press event. Seemed clear to me they are still holding Michael and Kara, anyway. My dad just wants the attention. If he's listening to my mom, then he believes that this whole shit storm will bring tourists to the mountain, rather than scare them off."

Bo's brow wrinkled, but she didn't answer. Carl had just walked out of the building and was coming toward them with his head down and a manila envelope tucked under one arm.

Keegan rolled his window down and accepted the thick packet without a word. Carl nodded and jogged back inside. Not even a wave.

"This seems sketchy," Bo remarked as Keegan peeled out of the parking lot and down a back road that would spit them near the lake.

He agreed. "Bo, why are we doing this?" They'd arrived at the far side of Hogtown, not a mile from the lake. Scrub brush and junipers had taken the places of pines and oaks out on the plains of Hogtown. He put the truck in park and shifted his weight.

She answered plainly enough. "To solve a homicide. To find and maybe save three missing people. To salvage Mary's reputation. I could go on . . ."

He held up a hand. "I mean they have Michael and Kara. They might have evidence we don't know about."

"How could Michael or Kara have kidnapped four people and hidden three of them in the span of hours? And where would he put them?"

Bo had opened the file and began combing through the contents.

"I don't know how to read this," she admitted. He peered over her shoulder as she paged through vaguely familiar report sections.

Bo held them up in defeat and rubbed her eyes. "You take a look. I'm frustrated."

Scratchy handwriting revealed a rushed medical examination. But the verdict was clear: Manner of death: murder. Cause of death: gunshot wound to the head. He translated the information to Bo and shuffled through the pages until he found more photographs and further notations.

According to the coroner's results, Joanie had been sprayed with a shot gun. Her wrists and ankles were bound postmortem. The bindings loosened, which may have accounted for her float up to the top of the lake. She may originally have been strapped to a boulder or brick. She definitely entered the water after the gunshot, which could have been any time between midnight and four in the morning. And that was a conservative window.

No sexual assault was suspected.

Keegan let out a breath. "Doesn't sound . . ." he began, searching for the right words.

"Like a heat-of-the-moment kind of thing?"

He snapped and locked eyes with her. "Exactly." She tucked a strand of hair behind her ear.

"If Michael killed her, it wouldn't have been impassioned. He'd have had to act fast. Maybe it'd have even been accidental."

"Michael said they had sex."

"But there was no clear evidence of rape. Maybe they did have DNA. I don't know. Is there any information about the scene of the crime? Where was she shot? Did they find blood at the lodge? Was it cleaned up?"

Keegan knew there was no way she was killed there. Plus, they didn't have any idea where Joanie and her friend group had wandered to between checking in at the lodge and the wee hours of July 5.

Keegan flashed back through the paperwork, coming up with half an answer. "Dawson's most recent report indicates there was no blood found at Wood Smoke. They found her purse near the shore, but they had only just started dragging the lake. Tire tracks at the lake match only those vehicles that were expected, including vehicles belonging to . . . officers called to the scene, Logan Zick, Paul Zick, Keegan Flanagan, and . . ." Keegan looked up at her, panic creasing his features. "Bob Flanagan."

CHAPTER 31

Bo cut in. "Your dad?"

Keegan took a breath and nodded.

He was clearly freaking out. She would, too, if she were him. A weak justification was all she could offer. "He's the mayor. It makes sense he'd be there. Maybe he was checking things out. And obviously the cops don't suspect him."

He shut the engine off and opened his door, leaving her in the truck. She debated following him, but thought better of it, instead returning to the envelope and digging a hand back inside.

Glossy photo paper smudged between her fingers as she pulled out the unedited close-ups. Each page had a ruler and a number.

Evidence.

She looked through the pages, carefully examining the mundaneness of it all. A leather purse. Designer. Heavy and sopping.

An interior shot of the purse. Darkened silk lining played backdrop to a mess of miscellany.

She set the page aside and turned to the next.

A set of car keys, glistening with lake water.

A compact, its corner chipped.

Chapstick.

Lip gloss.

A day planner, the pages bruised with runny ink.

A second key ring with a single key.

Bo was about to flip to the next photograph, but she stopped. Michael had her room key, still. Didn't he?

A second key ring. With a single key.

She threw her door open and screamed for Keegan to come back to the truck as she dropped the other photos to the floor of the truck and held the one closer to her face, looking hard at the wooden tag.

In the wood, deeply set, was the carving of a wolf. *A timber wolf.*

Thank God.

But it wasn't a fox. Or an elk. Or a squirrel or a bear.

It was a carnivorous, heinous wolf.

————

She didn't have to explain it. As soon as he saw, he agreed. Kara.

It had to be.

It made perfect sense. A theory formed and Bo had half a mind to call the police. She directed Keegan to downtown Maplewood, where she had a plan.

As they drove, she explained her theory. "Michael

hooks up with Brittany. Kara finds out. Maybe sees him. Kara freaks. Altercation ensues."

"What does this have to do with Joanie? Or the others?"

"Maybe they saw Michael or Kara hurt Brittany? Maybe Brittany is dead, too?"

"Why is Kara's room key in Joanie's purse?"

"I don't know."

Keegan rolled his eyes. She caught him and socked him softly on the shoulder. "If the cops are keeping Michael and Kara, then they have something. Meanwhile, they haven't found the others. I have an idea where to look."

Her stomach rumbled to life as they pulled down a new dirt road on the outskirts of town.

The Cabins.

It was the new luxury housing development. Bo was familiar with it because Kurt had bought a lot there just like Michael and Dutch. And now, everything came together. Michael's connection to the Delaneys. Mary, particularly. Kurt, specifically.

Michael was the architect on the project. Dutch, Anna's boyfriend, was the general contractor. This was the missing link; it had to be.

But, if Brittany didn't turn up soon- in the lake or else-where, then Bo would have to admit that she, just like the cops, had nothing. No answer.

CHAPTER 32

Keegan sank into the Delaney's sofa as he studied Michael.

"I gave the key to Brittany. No idea how Joanie got it."

Michael had been released on bond. His lawyers couldn't get him released from *Maplewood*, however; but now, the whole Delaney brood plus Michael and Kara were holed up in the Delaney farm on Ingleheart Lane.

After finding themselves stuck outside a locked gate and expansive perimeter fence at the Cabins, Keegan and Bo had given up. Bo admitted it was a long shot. A wild-goose chase. A red herring. She agreed to take a break and rejoin the family at the farm, where she and Keegan now sat, rapt, as Michael sipped on a cup of coffee next to his lawyer, who was adamantly opposed to Michael or Kara speaking to anyone.

The mere presence of Kara was enough to send Bo into a downward spiral of self-doubt. But she was holding it together nicely. Keegan felt proud of her. His girl was tough.

"Why did you give *Brittany* a room key? And, by the way, where is mine?" Bo asked.

Kara had left the house to reserve a guest room in the last available motel in Maplewood: Mountain Guest Cabins. They had one room available. No bed-and-breakfast would host Michael and Kara.

By that point, Kara's parents had settled down in Phoenix with the kids. Michael's parents lived in Vegas and wouldn't be coming.

All they had were the Delaneys. But still, Dick and Margaret said no to hosting the two. Not in their home. Not near their family. They could find a new motel and leave as soon as possible.

Now, they were just waiting for Kara to return and take her no-good husband with her. Michael had no qualms with sharing his story, even on record.

Bo took furious notes as Keegan studied the man. Keegan wasn't a murder detective, but he *was* a cop. The guy seemed smarmy but clean. His face was wan, eyes heavy. A two- or three-day-old outfit wrinkled along his skin as he rubbed his eyes and recounted his version to Bo, giving her full permission to publish whatever he said.

"You can't do that," the lawyer interjected. "It's an open case. You can't go on record about anything. Strike that." He slashed a finger at Bo's laptop.

"Off the record, fine. I can attribute to an anonymous source, cool?" She pointed the question to Michael rather than his waxed-and-tanned representative.

Michael agreed. "I want it out there. I can't have this on my reputation. I run a business. I have a family." He looked beyond Bo and toward the door. If Keegan didn't know better, he'd think the man was sorry. "I don't have time for a trial to clear my name."

"So, why did you give it to her?"

Keegan shifted next to Bo's slight frame. Hunger rumbled in his stomach.

Michael cleared his throat, pulled something from his pocket, and slid it across the table. Her room key. Perfectly fine. Dry. Innocent. Michael took another sip from his mug. "I told Brittany if her motel arrangement fell through that I'd extend my stay at the lodge." He glanced away and Keegan snorted.

"You were going to send Kara back to Phoenix and stay here to hook up with Kurt's ex in Mary's lodge?"

Bo flashed Keegan a grateful look before returning her eyes to her laptop and awaiting Michael's answer.

"I didn't *know* she was Kurt's ex, remember? You," he pointed at Bo, "told me she was a guest. *She* didn't say anything, either." He blew out a sigh and rubbed his hands across his face. "Look, I suck. I run around on Kara. But I'm not a killer. I never even saw those other guests!" His voice rose and his face flushed. The lawyer placed a hand on Michael's forearm.

"I think you've got the full account. Don't quote Mr. Erinhard. And don't quote me. If your piece is used in any way in court, you can expect a lawsuit."

He stood and nudged Michael to follow him out to the front deck.

Bo and Keegan stayed at the kitchen table while she reviewed her notes.

"I'm ready," she said, clicking into her email and attaching a file.

Keegan checked his watch as Dick Delaney came in from the backyard. "Sir." Keegan stood and nodded at the older man who returned his greeting in kind.

"Hi, Dad," Bo murmured before slapping her laptop shut and popping up. "We have to leave, again. Sorry, but I need more info."

Lunchtime had come and gone, and Keegan had to beg Bo to slow down long enough to grab a burger before barreling ahead to Maplewood Guest Cabins. She was ready to confront Kara, the woman who'd become her prime suspect, especially now in the wake of Michael acting like an innocent scumbag. Somehow.

But as they pulled into the parking lot of the Guest Cabins, Bo picked up the photographs from earlier.

She paused, moving through the photos. "Hang on, I hadn't finished looking at these," she told him.

Keegan looked out the windshield, his eyes open to catch Kara move in or out of the office or one of the shabby rooms.

"Keegan, look."

He glanced over to the photograph in her hand as she bent it toward him. "One of Mary's brochures." She pointed out.

He squinted at the image. The brochure's center pages were partially obscured by a rectangular overlay.

Bo's finger pressed down on the shape.

It was a business card. Maybe it had been tucked in to the brochure.

"Is that——?" Keegan began.

She finished his sentence, reading aloud from the eggshell-white paper, its milky ink barely legible. "Paul Zick, Editor-in-Chief. *Mountain Times*."

CHAPTER 33

By the time they'd made it to Bo's office, Paul wasn't there. Stewart had evaded Bo's questions, choosing not to reveal whether his brother had gone home for the day or elsewhere. So they packed it in, promising to return the next morning.

Now, here they were again, and Paul still hadn't shown up to work.

No press release from the cops. And the paper didn't go out on Sundays.

She told Keegan they had to find Paul. Then they were going to call Bob Flanagan. He left the office to pace the front sidewalk as she pressed Stewart from within her office.

In front of the entire newspaper staff, Bo dialed Paul's cell, but it went straight to voicemail. Sighing and tucking her phone into her back pocket, she turned again to her boss's brother. "Stewart, are you running my narrative?"

"Already did, Roberta," he assured her.

"Where's the copy?"

He strode behind the front desk to a stapled set and handed it over. "Here you go." His hands shook as he passed it her way, and his eyes darted behind her, searching, apparently, for Keegan.

Bo read through her report, looking for areas Paul may have edited.

Mayhem on the Mountain

Bo Delaney

Reporter, Mountain Times

The rural community of Maplewood, Arizona, is struck with fear. For the first time in over a century, a murderer lurks among us.

With the discovery of one sodden and shotgun-blazed body came confusion. But as details sewed themselves together, so too did a clearer picture. Four tourists. One dead. Three missing.

Police have pointed the finger of the law at an architect from Phoenix. Michael Erinhard. Though uncouth and philandering, he didn't do it. Evidence has shifted away from Michael. Still, any possible resolution to the case remains shrouded in mystery.

Is Michael's wife implicated?

Yes.

Did she kill four fellow Phoenicians?

No.

What you will read here is not my attempt to play policewoman. Not my effort to sleuth about and presume to investigate complicated and horrific events. But, instead, my observations.

Reader, take caution. What follows is controversial at best and slanderous at worst. However, when you're raised on a moun-taintop in ol' AZ, you have little other choice than to be honest.

Reader, if you live here, then you needn't read on. You already know this. If, however, you are a visitor. A summer tourist. A weekender. A second-home owner. A vacationer. Then be warned. It's not pretty.

Locals hate tourists.

July 4 is more than a holiday. It's more than an excuse to throw back beer and swallow down barbequed wieners.

July 4 is the anniversary of the founding of our nation. On this day, some of us stop to remember a time when certain princi-ples were asserted. The land wasn't new. But the people were.

July 4 is also, now, the day that kicked off Maplewood's most maddening news story to date. But murder on the mountain is no news story. It's a tragedy of worrying proportions.

I grew up on the mountain. I worked hard and played hard. I did my time. I also, unlike many locals, left the mountain. For over fifteen years, in fact. Exploring the flatlands below us brought me a degree of perspective. But what really opened my eyes wasn't living away from the mountain. Returning to the mountain did that.

Sure, when I was a teenager, I complained with everyone else. Noisy movie theaters. Litter-bound lakes. Clogged roads. I hated them, too.

And when I returned not three weeks ago, I hated them again. Other people come to our mountain and treat it like a cheap motel room.

I don't think a horny architect killed four people.
I don't think his scorned wife killed four people.
I think one of us killed four people.

————

He didn't change a damn thing.

CHAPTER 34

Keegan pressed his phone to his ear as he sat in the driver's seat of his truck. Bo was next to him, holding his hand atop the console.

After two rings, a voice came on the line.

"Dad?"

"Keegan, how's it going, son?"

"Do you have any new information on the investigation? Any trace of Brittany? The others?"

Bob murmured something away from the phone before returning. "Well, Keegan, I'm here with Brittany's parents now. They're upset, of course. One minute."

Keegan waited as his father presumably found a more private spot. Bob's voice had lost the effervescence of the preceding days. It was drawn and monotone. No lilting drawl. No false cheer. Or real cheer. He sounded, for once, like a father rather than a mayor.

"Son, they dragged the lake last night and are continuing this morning. The police have begun to expand their investigation and have called in some of our friends for questioning."

Friends? Keegan had no friends in common with his parents. "What do Brittany's parents make of this? Have there been any signs of her at all? Please, Dad. We're desperate for some information. People are scared. We need to know what's happening."

Bob cleared his throat and answered. "No signs of her. Cops expect more information to turn up soon. They think the other three have been killed. Is Bo still writing a story?"

"Yes, the office is running it first thing tomorrow. There will be an online clip published later today, I think." He glanced at Bo. Her eyebrows knitted together and she covered the top of his hand with her other one.

"Um, Keegan, I'm not sure that's such a fine idea."

Keegan scoffed. "What do you mean?"

"Keegan," the man began, pausing for effect. "Keegan, Paul was taken in for questioning last night."

"Did you find out why his tire tracks were found at the lake?" Bo asked once he'd finished the phone call and they began to drive to the Search and Rescue station. Keegan planned to petition to rejoin the case, now that he was further removed from any suspicion.

Keegan let out a sigh. "Obviously not. You heard the whole conversation." He pulled his hand away and slid it across the steering wheel as he turned onto the highway.

"Why not, though?"

A caravan of SUVs crawled past and Keegan pulled out

behind them. SOCCER MOM stickers and STUDENT OF THE MONTH decals flashed him from the back windshields of the dark vehicles.

"If I would have asked him, then he'd have known we saw the report."

"Who cares? He's your dad."

Keegan scratched his chin and considered this for a moment. He didn't have the sort of relationship with his father in which either one of them could be honest and open.

However, there was one other person they could call to get information. One person who was the main artery for Maplewood gossip. She might shine some light on Paul Zick's involvement even before they arrived at his office.

Victoria Flanagan.

He dialed his mom, who was happy to oblige.

"Keegan, I'm so glad you called. I was about to be in touch. I just heard the news."

Keegan quickly hit the speaker button and darted a glance to Bo. "What news, Mom?"

"They found Brittany's purse."

CHAPTER 35

They had pulled up to the station, but Keegan's mom wasn't quite done sharing her insider knowledge. When asked where she'd gleaned the information, she told them Detective Biggans and his wife had just bought a home from her. The two women had grown close enough to join each other for cocktails every Saturday at the Last Chance, and it just spilled out.

"The other thing I found out," she went on in a whispery voice over the speaker, "is that Michael and Kara had an agreement that he could sleep with other women."

Keegan shook his head and rolled his eyes. Bo let a smile lift her mouth and she waited for him to untangle himself from the phone call so that they could go inside and Keegan could make his case for jumping onto a search party.

After popping his door open, she began to follow suit, but he held a hand up. "It's better if I go alone."

Affronted, her face fell, but she nodded. She understood. Watching Keegan cross the parking lot into the office had returned her mind to her feelings for him. How they were growing and stalling. The case had consumed and sucked them down into the same black hole, where romance couldn't bloom. Too dark. She swallowed and fell back into her seat. After things settled, where would she and Keegan stand?

A vibration rattled her satchel to life and she dipped her hand inside to fish it out. Her family had begun a frantic group text, which Bo was generally ignoring. Now, she had time to scroll through.

Nothing more than mundane chatter.

Her eyes flashed to the top of the messaging app. No Keegan. She kept scrolling until she neared the most recent texts.

A message from Mary caught Bo's attention.

Have they found any other evidence? I heard somewhere they bagged a bunch of stuff from Wood Smoke . . .

Then, a light bulb flickered behind the brunette's eyes and she thought back to her trip to the lodge. She'd been in her room and Michael's. Nowhere else. She hadn't known the loud-mouthed college kids were involved. She completely ignored their room.

If they left just after check-in . . . then their luggage would have stayed behind. They hadn't checked out, so to speak. She and Keegan had looked through all the evidence photos his friend had passed over. But those hadn't included *everything*.

By now, the police definitely knew something. They knew what Joanie, Kat, and David had left behind.

Calling the station was useless. Victoria had given them all she had. Paul was detained. The only other options for info included Keegan's friend, Stewart, and Logan.

She knew Logan would never talk. He was crazy and useless. Completely irate that a murder scene was unfolding in his backyard. All he wanted was to get on with his moaning and groaning and fishing.

Hopefully, Keegan would soon spill out from the Search and Rescue headquarters with ample information and a direct line to the detectives' ears and mouths.

If not . . .

Stewart was an option. Bo could sidle up to him. Flirt. Kiss ass.

She wondered if Joanie's folks were at the station. Answering questions and sobbing into snotty tissues over weak paper cups of coffee.

Wait a minute.

Keegan emerged, his head hung and his hands shoved into his pockets.

She popped the door and stood on the running board and waved. "Keegan! We have to go back to the Mountain Guest Cabins!" She hollered across the square gravel lot.

He glanced around himself and jogged to the truck, jumping inside and holding a hand to his mouth to shush her. "Why? I thought we agreed to rule Kara out?" His voice was low. Irritation marked his face.

"Not for Kara," Bo answered, closing her door and strapping herself in. Her heart had begun to race. "For Brittany's parents."

CHAPTER 36

"We can't just barge in and start questioning them about their missing daughter," Keegan reasoned without starting the engine.

Bo grabbed his arm and pinned him with a look. She breathed in and out and held his gaze. "You're not back on the case, are you?"

He shook his head.

"Is it because you're . . ." she searched for the right phrase, landing uncomfortably on, "*with me?*"

He rubbed his hands over his face and when it emerged, a smile gripped his mouth. He looked at her. "Yeah." Anger, frustration, disappointment . . . none of it filled his voice.

She retrieved the apology that had sat on her brain since Keegan was first given the boot. "I'm so sorry, Keegan." Her eyes dropped to her lap with her hands, but he reached over and cupped her chin in his palm.

"Bo, I don't care."

Cheeks flushing, Bo moved a hand and hooked it on his wrist. She didn't know what to say.

He didn't seem to mind, because he moved across the cab, pressed his mouth to hers, combed his fingers through her hair, and drew himself in for a deep kiss.

She kissed him back, her anxieties melting out of the truck and into the cool morning, where they would twist themselves among the pine trees and over felled pine cones and try hard to vanish entirely.

But as soon as Keegan pulled back, those anxieties sucked themselves back through the window of the truck, filling her chest again. Tears clouded her eyes and she tried hard to swallow them down.

"Bo, what is it?"

A fat droplet spilled over her lower lash line. Keegan rubbed it from her cheek with his thumb and dropped his hand to hold hers.

"Keegan, I have to help solve this case. I'm the reason there is a case to begin with. If I'd just let Kurt deal with his own skeletons, things would be totally different."

"Maybe. Maybe not. We don't know when Joanie and her friends went missing. Maybe it was before Brittany. Maybe you had nothing to do with it, Bo." He returned his hand to cover hers. "Listen, every law enforcement officer on the mountain is working it. They'll figure it out. We don't have to, Bo. We could go back to my place. Take a nap. Grab a bite to eat. Wait it out. If we can manage to lay low, they may even put me back on the case eventually."

She reared her head back. "You don't want to be associated with me?"

"No, no, no." He backpedaled, almost physically, pulling his hand away and holding both palms up to stop her. "I just don't see how we can possibly push on. We've exhausted our sources. The evidence is locked up. I don't know if I can get my connection to leak more, and I really don't know if I want to go there at this point."

She wiped the almost-tears from her eyes. "Wait, Keegan. No, we haven't. Brittany's parents. We have to try to talk to them."

Keegan studied her. "They won't talk to you."

She thought about it for a moment. An idea flickered. "Well, maybe not. But put yourself in the shoes of someone whose daughter is missing. They don't know if she's dead. We don't either. They want to find out. If I knew someone who went missing, I would do whatever it took to find them."

Keegan pulled his keys from his pocket and inserted one into the ignition.

Bo reached her own hand to cover his as she batted her eyelashes up at him.

"And, Sheriff Flanagan, of all people trying to help, I would think they'd be most apt to talk to a gritty local reporter and her well-meaning sidekick."

CHAPTER 37

Normalcy.

Keegan missed it.

He missed waking up, hitting the lake for his miles. Coffee. Office banter. Hiking. Searching. Rescuing.

If everything went back to normal, however, he wouldn't be satisfied. Now that Bo had filled his days, he couldn't imagine going back to normal. Yes, he wanted the killer to be found. Yes, he desperately hoped Brittany and Kat and David were alive and well and would recover from whatever horrific experience they'd undergone.

But he wanted Bo. Badly.

He followed her command and drove down to the Guest Cabins off the highway. It was a shabby motel, especially compared to Wood Smoke Lodge.

Maplewood offered nothing ritzy. Those who had money and wanted a nice place to stay on the mountain typically bought their own. Those who didn't want a regular thing stayed at Mary's lodge.

The Guest Cabins were for college kids who couldn't

afford the lodge or locals who bargained with the owner to rent out a room on a weekly or biweekly basis.

So, when Bo rapped her little knuckles on room one, where they suspected the Purcells could be found (thanks to a five dollar bribe for the desk clerk), it was no surprise that one eye peered out of the crack below the chain.

"Mr. Purcell?" Bo asked.

His voice was soft. Unassuming. Calm. A one-eighty from what Bo and Keegan would have expected. Keegan looked around, surprised by the lack of a security detail. There might be an undercover tucked low behind the steering wheel of one of the vehicles in the parking lot. If so, he was either asleep or unwilling to reveal himself over Keegan and Bo's presence.

"My name is Bo Delaney," she began. He wasn't sure what her plan was for coaxing herself into their room. She went on, ad-libbing smoothly. "I work at Wood Smoke Lodge. I saw your daughter before she went missing."

Moments later, they were inside the room, standing awkwardly next to a faux wooden desk.

Keegan had been in the Guest Cabins on various assignments for work. He hadn't had as much of a chance to reflect on their interior design.

Mr. and Mrs. Purcell stood in stark contrast to the dated room. Mrs. Purcell perched on the edge of the bed in an outfit not unlike what Keegan's own mother would wear. Her hair was done. Her makeup set. French tips peeked out from her fingers. Her hands folded in her lap. She seemed to be expecting someone.

Mr. Purcell was dressed in Dockers and a polo. His hair was gelled back and his tan skin radiated as he crossed his arms over his fit chest and leaned back against a wood-paneled wall on the far side of the room.

Nothing fit together.

His wan voice. Their clean-cut affects. The dark room with furniture straight out of 1982. A tube television sunk into a particle board dresser. Antennae sprung forth from its back end.

Introductions were over. Keegan cleared his throat in the quiet room. "Mr. and Mrs. Purcell, I can imagine the stress you're under."

They nodded solemnly.

He went on. "We are not officially with the investigation because of the conflict of interest." He waved a hand at Bo, who glared at him subtly. He licked his lips, forging ahead and keeping his eyes on her. "We want to be upfront and honest."

Mrs. Purcell sniffed.

"I have significant experience in search and rescue, and Bo is a solid journalist. We think we might have an important question to ask you which could lead the authorities to Brittany. If anything sticks, we will take it to them and pursue it to the maximum of our capacity."

Bo looked up at him, her lips in a tight line.

Mr. Purcell studied Keegan before asking, "If you two are such professionals, then why aren't you working the case? What is this? A vigilante operation?"

Bo cracked a smile and answered for Keegan. "Frankly, sir . . . Yes, it is."

Mrs. Purcell's face relaxed, to Keegan's surprise, and she invited them to sit in the two chairs by the desk.

Keegan sank onto the threadbare upholstered seat and gripped his knees. "Bo? You want to start?"

Bo bent down to pull something out of her satchel. Keegan expected her laptop, but instead, it was the manila envelope.

He monitored their expressions as Bo hesitated and met Mrs. Purcell's sad gaze.

"Mrs. Purcell, I know you've probably been shown some of this evidence, and we are not technically allowed . . . "

Keegan put a hand on her knee. "Bo, let me." She stared at him with a crinkled brow. "I'm going to take responsibility for this, okay?" She nodded at him and glanced toward Brittany's parents. He went on. "We came by this piece of evidence without explicit permission from the police department. But we feel it could answer some questions, at least for now."

Mrs. Purcell looked back at her husband and wrung her hands. He answered for them both. "Go on."

"Were you asked to identify Brittany's purse?"

CHAPTER 38

"Asked to identify her purse? No," Mrs. Purcell choked out. Her eyes grew watery and she covered her mouth with her hand. Behind her, Mr. Purcell moved from the far wall. He joined his wife on the sofa and wrapped an arm around her waist. He locked eyes with Bo and nodded for her to continue.

Again, Keegan cut in. Bo was thankful for the moment he offered. She didn't quite know how to show them the picture. The picture that may or may not mean Brittany was dead. The picture that may or may not confirm that the place in which Joanie's body was pulled from was the same place in which Brittany's purse was recovered.

She swallowed and Keegan held up both his hands. "We don't know where Brittany is. This photo may or may not tell us. You have to be ready for the possibility that Brittany is dead."

To her surprise, Mr. and Mrs. Purcell did not react to this admission. Mrs. Purcell did not bury her face in her husband's shoulder. Tears did not splash from her eyes. Neither one of them turned defensive.

Instead, Mr. Purcell launched into a story that would forever change Bo's opinion of Brittany. A story that would gratify Bo in her choice to help the drunken woman. A story that would resolve any bad feelings Bo had for Kurt.

"Brittany has been struggling since the divorce," he began as his wife nodded beside him. "She'd been cheating on Kurt and looking for a way out of the marriage. We'd pushed her too hard to have it all: a career, a husband, a family. In fact, she wanted none of it. Except, maybe, the career. Her marriage to Kurt lasted as long as it did simply because he is a good man. He put up with a lot. Once he left her, she was crushed. She came to realize she never quite worked out what she wanted. Once she lost it all, she went off the deep end."

Mrs. Purcell took over. "She told us she was going to win Kurt back and resurrect her perfect life. Have a child. But she began drinking. Once she learned about his engagement, she plotted her trip up here for the very next holiday. I found a tidy little to-do list soon after we reported her missing. She thought of everything, including a fake pregnancy test to scare away his poor fiancée." Mrs. Purcell pressed her fingers into the hollows beneath her brow bone. "I'm so sorry for all the trouble Brittany has caused. And I wish I were surprised. We knew she was in bad shape. We didn't know she was willing to take her life in her own hands."

Bo considered what Brittany's parents had shared. Did they think she was dead? Did they think she would have killed herself?

Keegan cleared his throat next to her. "I'm sorry to hear your daughter was struggling so much. She may still be alive, you know."

They nodded sadly before looking at each other. A secret seemed to pass between them.

Bo picked up the photo of the lake-soaked leather purse and flipped it around to face them. "Mr. and Mrs. Purcell, is this Brittany's purse?"

Mrs. Purcell's eyes widened and then closed. She opened them once more and looked at Bo. "Yes. I'm sure of it."

Bo suspected there were some loose strings within the investigation. But this was a gaping hole. The key wasn't in Joanie's purse. It was in Brittany's purse. Michael hadn't lied.

And the brochure and Paul's business card were in Brittany's purse. Not good for Paul. Bo wondered if he was still at the station, fielding the same questions she had just two days before.

"Was it found in the same lake as that other girl? The younger one?" Mr. Purcell asked, his face drawn.

Keegan confirmed that it was.

Finally, Mrs. Purcell broke down. Heaving sobs wracked her slender body and shook the cheap double bed beneath her. Mr. Purcell hugged and held her.

Bo felt like shit. She might as well have told Brittany's parents that Brittany was dead. She'd lose her job, for sure. Keegan might lose his.

But then, Mr. Purcell asked something that would distract Bo from the consequences of her decision. Something that would twist a knife into her working theory about Paul and her secret theory about Keegan's dad.

"Do you think it was Brittany?"

Keegan frowned. "What do you mean?"

Mrs. Purcell choked out a last sob and answered for her husband. "Do you think Brittany killed them?"

CHAPTER 39

They shut themselves into Keegan's truck. A shiver ran through Keegan's body as he started the engine. "Where are we going?"

Defeat was beginning to sink in. He didn't think Brittany, a woman of slight build and compromised mental faculties, could have managed to accost and kill three grown people then successfully disappear OR drown herself.

"Let's stop at your place for a break. I need to wrap my head around everything. Maybe write another piece and send it to Stewart. Or Paul, if he's released."

Keegan pulled onto the highway after a mob of motorcycles vroomed past. "You don't suspect Paul?"

"Yes, I do suspect Paul. But I'm starting to suspect *everyone*. Aren't you? No wonder the police have butterfingers on this case. No one and everyone has a motive and an alibi."

"How do you mean?" Keegan asked.

He turned left up the mountain and toward his place

by the lake. A shower and a mug of coffee would wake him up. Her, too, with any luck. He glanced over to Bo and she launched into her rundown, which wasn't too dissimilar from his.

"Michael and Kara. I was nearly certain it was Kara until I started writing that piece, when it dawned on me that the timing didn't add up. She had no opportunity to hunt down the three others, right?"

"We don't know that. She could have killed them earlier on July fourth. She and Michael both. We don't know where they were before they showed up for check-in, after all."

She nodded in agreement. "Okay, so why would they kill three strangers? That would make for some dark serial killer shit."

Bo was right. Serial killer shit, indeed. Which made no sense. But he wasn't ruling either of them out. Kara was odd. She didn't fit with the suave, smooth-talking architect. Her mousy hair and dull skin practically disintegrated when she wilted next to Michael's fake tan and Chiclet teeth.

Bo let out a sigh and pulled the evidence envelope out of her satchel. "Michael didn't lie. He admitted to sleeping with her. He gave her a key. If he were going to kill her, why give the cops such damning evidence?"

"He could say he was framed."

"But he didn't."

"No," Keegan admitted.

"We still don't know if Kara knew about their hook-up."

"We can assume she had an inkling, especially after

what she told me when I took her back to the lodge." He glanced over to see Bo squinting at the photograph with the brochure and business card.

"If this was in Brittany's purse and *she* put it in there, then how did she get it? When would she have run into Paul?"

Keegan frowned. "Last Chance. He was there with my dad. I saw them both. I *avoided* them both, in fact."

The entire truck seemed to shift as Bo's body whiplashed at his revelation. "Your dad was at the bar?"

Easing on the gas as he turned down the lane toward his place, he gripped the steering wheel and focused ahead. "Yeah? So?"

———

It was their first argument since being stuck together for three days.

Mayor Bob Flanagan—his *father*—a murder suspect in Bo's mind. Once he'd parked the truck, he killed the engine and strode inside. Away from her. She didn't follow.

After throwing together a pot of coffee and chucking a bagel into the toaster, he withdrew his cell and dialed his mom.

Once it began ringing, something pulled inside him. He moved to the front window and stared out. Bo was no longer perched on the front seat of his truck. She wasn't just outside his truck. She wasn't making her way up his deck. She was nowhere.

"Hello?"

"Mom, hi," he answered, his eyes flashing through the window as far as he could see. "Where's Dad?"

Victoria Flanagan usually relished the act of sharing a hot piece of gossip.

Not today.

Keegan could practically hear her wringing her hands and pacing across the cowhide rug that anchored her bed. "Detective Dawson called an hour ago. Your father has to do another press conference."

A flash of dark hair came into his view of the deck.

"Why? Did they find something new?"

Bo cracked the door and interrupted. "The police dragged the lake—"

Just as she was about to finish her sentence, his mom answered him, her enthusiasm for mountain excitement long gone. In its place, fear.

"Keegan, they found more bodies."

CHAPTER 40

Keegan and Bo had rushed from his cabin to the station, where they met his dad and Paul.

Paul had been released from questioning under the same circumstances as Bo. In the lobby of the police station, he stood, his face white. Bob conferred with Detectives Dawson and Biggins on how to proceed with the conference, which would happen at the station this time as opposed to the town square or any other beautiful gathering spot.

Bo pulled Paul aside. "What's going on? Why did they question you?" Having the upper hand, she was able to pin him in a corner of mismatched plastic waiting room chairs.

He kept his eyes trained on Bob and shook his head. "Not sure. I had to tell them again about when Logan called me that morning. Go over the phone call, all that. Cops have no effing clue who to blame."

Bo ignored his nervous behavior and pressed on. "Paul, did they find Brittany? Is that the new body?"

Paul shrugged and drew a hand to his mouth, chewing furiously on a hangnail.

Changing tactics, she asked him the one question that had been on her mind since she'd inspected the evidence photographs. She was beyond caring about whether she'd get in trouble. After digging in her satchel, she shifted the envelope so that it was hidden in front of her body and shielded away from the others.

"Paul," she whispered, pulling out the photograph in question. "Why did Brittany have your business card?"

His eyes scanned the photo. Once he recognized his familiar eggshell-white card, his face opened and he looked at Bo. "Where did you get that?"

"Just answer me. The cops have this, too. Did they ask you about it?"

He rubbed a hand over his mouth and nodded sadly before grabbing her elbow. Roughly, he pushed her down a side hall and into the nook near the water fountain.

Once he'd peeked around her at the others, he lowered his voice and locked eyes with her. "Bo," he began. She took note of the fact that this moment, this moment in the middle of a damn murder case, was the moment he chose to finally use her nickname. "I told the cops everything I know. You have to believe me."

Her eyebrows wrinkled and she leaned in. "What do you know, Paul?"

Peering around her again, he shifted his weight back into the cubby behind the water fountain. "I met her. I met Brittany. At Last Chance. She was drunk. Really drunk. Bob was with me. I wasn't sure if she had friends to take care of her. I gave her my card. That's it, I swear, Bo. You have to believe me."

Desperation took the form of sweat beads along his hairline. The handsome older man turned into a pitiful middle-aged jerk before her eyes.

She turned to check on Keegan, who was huddled together with his father and Dawson. Biggans stood off to the left, studying his phone.

Looking back at Paul, a new question took shape. "So did she call you?"

"No, I mean . . . I don't think so. I didn't have any missed calls, after all. You see, we left the bar early in the night. Kathy was waiting for me at home. You can ask her. I made it there and went to bed."

He was treating her like a cop. Or the editor-in-chief. Not like a lowly reporter whom he'd just recently placed on leave.

Again, Bo looked back at the others, her eyes falling heavily on Bob Flanagan. *Mayor* Flanagan.

The man who was excited for media coverage.

The man who gallantly and enthusiastically headed up an initial press conference.

The man who now wilted next to his grown son. Who continued to throw furtive glances between the receptionist, Bo, Paul, and the men who were trying to make plans with him.

Leaving Paul to sip from the water fountain and dab at his forehead, Bo whipped around and joined Keegan and Bob. Matching in height and build, you could almost mistake them for twins from behind. If it weren't for Bob's silvery hair.

"Hey," Keegan said, closing his shoulder to her and clearing his throat.

Dawson paused mid-sentence. Bob glanced down at Bo. She raised her eyebrows. "Anything I can do?" she asked.

Biggans joined them with Paul looming over his shoulder.

"Ma'am, we appreciate you and Mr. Zick and your interest in the case. But it's highly inappropriate for the press to join this dialogue. You both can wait out front. We'll get rolling shortly."

Bo looked to Keegan, but he ignored her. Still pissed about her light accusation toward his father, no doubt.

Without a word, she left the circle.

Paul spilled out of the building soon after.

A crowd had begun to form with Heather-with-Channel-Five leading the mob to journalistic triumph. Bo had to take advantage of getting close to Paul while she could.

After all, it sounded as though he was rather pertinent to the investigation.

Being outside was good for Paul. He needed the fresh air, apparently. His color returned as he swept his sweat up into coiffed, silvery hair that stood above his tanned forehead. He offered her a half-smile as they stood awkwardly together, like a team. Bo grew aware of her outfit, her own jeans and T-shirt from the party, which Keegan had washed for her.

The lodge was still closed for the investigation, despite a distinct lack of useful evidence stemming from the singular locale.

Bo's mind flashed back to her brief search. Finding the

brochures. Cross-referencing them later and coming up empty-handed.

They had felt so relevant at the time. Like a cardstock clue, propped on the dresser, a code ready for Bo to crack.

The station doors opened, and out walked Keegan, Bob, and the two detectives. A receptionist scurried behind them with paperwork flashing from between cherry-red nails.

Heather-with-Channel-Five directed one of her lackeys to adjust the single microphone that wobbled on poorly mown grass, which spread from the police station to the highway.

Keegan moved away from her microphone and stood off to the side, examining the crowd as though he was no longer on her team. As though he was a cop again. A sheriff. And she was just his little brother's high school girlfriend.

She glared at him, though he never once looked toward her. Grimacing, she tried to focus on what the mayor had begun to say.

His voice grave, Bob Flanagan sounded different than before. Worried. He offered a quick review of previous events then introduced Detective Dawson to share developments of the case.

"Good afternoon, everyone. We understand your concerns and fears regarding the incidents at Hogtown Lake, and we want to assure you that every safety precaution is being taken to prevent further tragedy. Detective Biggans and I are following up on countless tips thanks to dutiful citizens such as yourselves. We cannot disclose information on suspects at this time, but we do regret to inform you that further discoveries have been made at Hogtown Lake."

Paul snorted beside her. "No info on suspects because they don't have any."

She frowned and strained to hear what else Dawson had to say.

"Apache County Search and Rescue dredged the lake. Unfortunately, they discovered two more bodies."

CHAPTER 41

Keegan locked eyes with Bo. Her face had gone sheet-white and she seemed to sink away from the crowd, falling back toward the narrow sidewalk that divided them from the highway.

Dawson continued with admonitions about locking doors and keeping aware, but Keegan stopped listening. He knew his father was innocent. He needed Bo to believe that. Because if she really thought the Maplewood Mayor was a serial killer, then she didn't belong on the mountain.

And if his father was, in fact, a serial killer, then Keegan couldn't see what his future would hold.

Up until now, chasing a murderer had been . . . fun, for lack of a better way to describe it. Teaming up with the enigmatic, dark-haired Delaney had awoken in him excitement the likes of which his job had never shown him. Irony, he supposed.

Then she had to go and ruin it by throwing the shadow of suspicion on his father. Keegan understood it. Both his parents enjoyed the thrill of news coverage and intrigue, however macabre. That his dad was so close to Paul didn't help things.

But what motive would his father have to kill three tourists? Or four?

In front of him, the crowd began to scatter. He caught sight of his father tucking his hands into his pockets and searching the crowd, probably for Paul, when the pretty reporter approached him.

Curious, Keegan stepped back and pulled out his phone, pretending to busy himself with text messages. He glanced toward the street to see Bo had disappeared. Torn between searching for her and eavesdropping on his father, he decided to do both and tapped out a quick text to Bo.

Behind him, Heather introduced herself privately to his dad. Her crew was packing up. She stood with Bob, alone. No microphone. Or camera.

His phone gripped tightly in his hand, he strained to hear.

"Does the detective think the killer is local?"

A pause.

Quiet giggling.

"Drinks? Off the record, of course."

He whipped around to see his father press his hand into Heather's lower back and guide her to the parking lot.

That wasn't the worst part, though. The worst part was when Bob Flanagan looked behind to Keegan and flashed a grin and a wink at his son.

CHAPTER 42

Bo didn't have a vehicle. So, she followed Paul, convinced she'd get something out of him, even if it was only a ride.

Once they stood in the back parking lot next to his Ford Bronco, she stalled, praying for Keegan to reappear, absolve her of whatever he thought she had done wrong.

Paul opened the passenger side door, waving her inside. She was welcome to join him back at the office until she could get a ride of her own. Bo looked around. No sign of Keegan.

She got inside.

After buckling her seatbelt and situating her satchel at her feet, Bo took stock of her boss's ride, which was impeccably clean. If it weren't for the giveaway boxy frame and two-toned exterior paint job (which had to have been touched up recently), she'd have guessed it was brand new.

Neither cigarette smoke nor mildewy mustiness filled her lungs as she heaved herself onto the passenger seat. No dust coated his dash. No grime ringed the inside of his cup holders. The upholstered seat bounced beneath her instead of deflating like a tired pool raft.

Paul and Logan were so *different* from each other.

"Um, how's your brother handling this whole thing?" He should expect the question. After all, he was a reporter, too.

Bo monitored Paul as he combed a hand through his hair then ran it along his jaw. Paul Zick was the epitome of dashing. It was no wonder he and Bob were buddy-buddy. Together, they looked more like handsome older brothers than Paul and Logan ever could.

A sigh preceded his answer. "Not well. He's been in and out of the station, too. Frankly, I'm worried about his health."

At that, Bo lifted her eyebrows. Sure, Logan was evidently in his sixties. But he was fit as a fiddle. Strong, too. Had to be for living off the grid. "What do you mean? Is he . . . sick or something?"

"Not exactly sick. Logan has always struggled with other people. You have to know that. When the rest of us moved out of Hogtown, he took it hard. Like a betrayal. We weren't betraying him or our father. We wanted a better life. Now, we have it. Logan can't handle it. It's gotten worse over the years."

It all made sense.

A red stoplight glowed ahead, and Bo realized the afternoon was growing long. Was she going to stay at her parents? Her pocket vibrated and she pulled out her phone.

Keegan. Asking if she wanted to link back up.

Then a second text, the more recent. He wanted to see

her. To talk. Blood pumped to her face, flushing her and distracting her from the awkward drive with Paul, who cleared his throat and interrupted a freshly formed daydream of spending one more night with Keegan.

"When Logan found the first body, he was in shock." Paul looked out his window, and Bo watched his hands as they twisted on the steering wheel. They were big hands. Dark and vascular. The fingernails clipped short and impossibly clean. They surely weren't the soft hands of a desk jockey, as her dad would say.

Bo kept her eyes on him until the light turned green and the car accelerated ahead.

"Is that why you showed up at the lake during the investigation?"

He nodded slowly but didn't say anything. She pressed on.

"Paul, did you ever think Logan might have had something to do with it?"

He didn't flinch at her question and instead knocked the blinker on. The offices of the *Maplewood Mountain Times* came into view as they crested a gradual hill and veered off the highway and into the squat front parking lot. Paul set the car into park but didn't move. Instead, he scratched his chin and shifted his weight to finally look at her.

"Of course not. Logan is mean but harmless." He licked his lips. "My turn to ask a question." He pinned her with his eyes, which were as light as hers. Piercing. Uncomfortable. She swallowed hard and sucked in a breath before nodding up at her boss, who covered her hand in his and opened his mouth to continue. "Bo, I admire your focus and dedication to the case. And I'm excited to see how you continue your personal narrative. I think. . ." He paused and glanced beyond her out the window. "I think you have a bright future in this business."

A frown pulled at her face. Where was this going? Curious, she nodded for him to continue.

"You know, Stewart wants to retire. We'll need a second-in-command by the end of summer, I think." He flicked a glance toward the office. Bo followed his gaze to the doors of the building. No opening or closing. No flashing of movement from within the small building. The Bronco's shiny paint job bounced off the glass and back at her. She returned her face to Paul. A strand of her hair fell onto her face. Paul lifted his hand from hers and reached over to tuck it behind her ear. "Why don't we discuss this over dinner?"

Everything about the last few days ran through her mind, but especially the photo wedged within her satchel. Brittany's purse. His business card. Slimy Bob Flanagan and his appearance at the bar *with* Paul.

And now, stupid, stupid Paul thought Bo was wooable. Bo, who was a good twenty years his junior. Bo, who was smarter than the average bear. Bo, whose ancestors had a bone to pick with Paul's ancestors.

And, apparently, Logan's.

In a moment, she made her decision.

"I'd love to."

They pulled out of the lot and Paul drove them back up the highway.

Away from *most* of Maplewood.

"Where are we going?" Bo asked. Other questions

formed in her mind; namely, why the business card? What did he say to Brittany? What did she say to him? Why was Bob Flanagan such a skeez? Did he pass those qualities onto his offspring?

"Jimmy Jake's." His tone fell off and Bo glanced over. Jimmy Jake's was a tourist trap. Shitty, overcooked meat and rubbery desserts.

But she nodded and studied him for a moment. His aquiline profile. Relatively taut skin and clear eyes. For a Zick, he wasn't hardened. She tried to picture Logan in Paul. If Logan had joined his family and moved, would he be good-looking, too?

Her phone buzzed in her pocket. Bo pulled it out and considered replying to Keegan, despite his pouty attitude. But it was a new text from Mary, which was more important.

Cops came back to question Kurt, Michael, and Kara again?! Do you know anything? Call me ASAP. Freaking out . . .

Paul slowed at the stoplight. Bo cleared her throat. "Um, do you know anything about the investigation? My sister just said the cops are back onto Kurt and Kara and Michael. The original suspects. They were cleared, though."

He kept his eyes ahead and accelerated through the light, turning left down Hogtown Lane.

Away from Jimmy Jake's.

CHAPTER 43

"Why did you turn?" Bo asked.

Paul looked over at her, sliding his hands along the clean leather of his steering wheel. "I have an idea. Bear with me, okay?"

She'd gone along with him thus far in order to dig up something for her next piece. She didn't want to be sitting in Paul's truck. She wanted to get back together with Keegan and keep at it. Write the next piece that would sell thousands of copies. Find the killer. Find Brittany.

"Listen, Paul, I have to be honest. I don't really want to go to dinner with you. I want to get back to work on the case."

His eyes lit up and he shook his head. "That's exactly what we're doing, trust me."

She pulled out her phone and began to reply to Mary as he continued.

"If the cops are with your guests—er, *former* guests— then the lake should be easy to access, right? Why don't we go have a look around? We can discuss our findings over a steak afterward."

It was as good an idea as any. But then again . . . "Don't you have easy access to the lake anyway? I mean with Logan basically living there?"

Paul seemed to consider that, which afforded her time to text Mary that she was going to find out. Because she was with Paul.

"I know this is going to upset you, Roberta," he finally answered. Bo's heart stopped. She trained her eyes on the road ahead. The world shrunk around her. The cabin of the truck felt hot. She pulled at her collar before her hand crawled to the door. He looked over at her and chuckled. "Whoa, calm down, girl." Paul reached his hand over and awkwardly patted her forearm. All her prior perceptions of a silver fox evaporated. She met his gaze as they neared Hogtown Lake.

"What's going to upset me?"

"Roberta—er, Bo—the cops found something that has forced them to return their attention to Kara, and there may be loose talk about Kurt, too."

Bo frowned. "What did they find? What do you mean?" And, she thought, if that were true, then she should be back at the station digging for this elusive piece of evidence. Not combing the lake.

Paul shook his head. "Something about a room key?" He avoided her gaze and instead pointed ahead to the lake and waved his hand ahead of them. She followed his hand to the tree-lined water. A rotting dock. Weeds. "That's where your story is, Roberta. Right here. The original settlement. The original Maplewood."

Bo saw no sign of an investigation. For having just dragged the lake and discovered more bodies, the place was deserted. Not even Heather-Coleman-with-Channel-Five or her news-crew groupies were around.

A face flashed in the window of Logan's crumbling cabin. Bo's eyebrows fell and she clicked her phone to life. "I'm not sure what you mean," she began, ready to dial Keegan to come pick her up.

Paul rested a hand on her arm. "Haven't you read Walden? Thoreau?"

Bo had. What that had to do with solving a triple—maybe quadruple—homicide was beyond her. She said as much.

"Let me ask you this. Who do you think killed those three?"

Bo shrugged, uncertain about revealing her cards.

"A tourist? A local?"

She considered his second question and tried to shift her arm out from beneath his hand. "I thought for a long time it might be Kara. Now, I'm not so sure."

It was funny. For the last few days, Bo felt she had no idea who was responsible for the tragedies. But now, as Paul sat next to her, his eyes reflecting the Hogtown sunset, she knew who she *didn't* suspect.

"I understand you dislike the mayor, which strikes me as surprising considering your growing relationship with Keegan."

Her eyebrows furrowed, and she opened her mouth to correct him but thought better of it. Her hands were free to tap out a text to Keegan, but something caught in her and she waited.

Paul, whose fingers still rested on the console to her side, turned in his seat and gave her a hard look. "I gave you a chance, Roberta."

Her head swiveled to meet his gaze. "A chance for what?"

"A chance to write the truth."

CHAPTER 44

Keegan's phone rang just as he was pulling up to the parking lot outside of the *Mountain Times*.

Bo.

He answered, relieved to hear her voice. "Hey."

She launched into a messy tale. She and Paul had visited Hogtown Lake. Got into an argument. She had accused his dad of acting suspiciously. She had accused Paul of some loose connection. Paul flew off the handle and left her at the lake to get her own ride. Bo said he was seething. All he had ever wanted was a personal narrative. The truth, she said he'd told her.

"Keegan, I have no freaking idea what the truth is. But I can tell you one thing—Paul is a nut job."

He slowed her down, asking her where she was. Still at the lake, walking and thinking. He told her that he'd head over to pick her up, to which she'd joked, "Thank God. I mean, if I had a fishing pole, I probably wouldn't mind just sitting out here and thinking. I don't know how Logan does it."

"Is he there?" Keegan asked, growing more nervous by the minute.

"I don't know. Did you hear that Kurt and Michael and Kara are back on the cops' radar?"

He turned onto the highway before realizing his gas tank was nearly empty. Keegan wasn't the type to let his gas tank get low. He kept it at or above half-full all the time. Every day. No exceptions.

He'd been distracted. "Yeah, I did hear. They are revisiting the photographs. Michael's room key. Some cell records they trudged up from months ago. I guess the investigation is stalled out. They are focusing almost solely on Brittany. And," he paused as he checked over his shoulder to change lanes and swing into Circle K, "I don't get why they don't seem to be too concerned with the first three dead kids."

"Keegan, oh my God," Bo answered. Her voice grew louder then turned muffled. He waited before pulling up to the available nozzle.

"Bo, are you okay? Should I call 911?"

"No, no, no. I'm fine. There's no one here. I just had an idea." Her voice had returned to normal and he could hear her shuffle papers on the other end.

He pulled up to the nozzle and descended from the truck, his phone wedged between his ear and shoulder. "Go on," he directed.

"Keegan, what were those kids up to earlier in the day? Where were they going? Did they go out to eat? Go for a hike?"

He muttered that the cops had probably covered those bases.

"No," she replied sharply. "I'm looking at Mary's brochure. Do you know what my sister lists as a local attraction?"

"No?"

"Fishing."

He scratched his jaw before tapping in his zip code for credit card authentication. "So?"

"Keegan, they came to Hogtown Lake before Brittany even showed up at the bar."

CHAPTER 45

Bo awoke at a kitchen table. A bowl of slop simmered in front of her as she lifted her head off the grimy oaken surface. Her chest ached and a searing pain shot through her neck when she tried to stand. The smell of bacon churned her stomach as she stifled a gag.

Ragged rope dug into her wrists and ankles. At first, Bo didn't realize it, but she slowly came to learn that she was tied up. Her hands strung through the slats of a wobbly wooden chair and knotted severely together. Each ankle firmly roped to its respective chair leg.

Bo took a breath and allowed her eyes to adjust to the dark room. The drip of a faucet rang out from a pot at the sink, which held no other dishes. The countertops were clear of anything, really. But the walls teamed with stuffed game—big and small. Fish frozen in mid-swim hung amongst the dried-out coats of rabbits and stags. Each animal more desperate than the last.

She squinted through to the far side of the room, trying to remember where she had been just before she awoke. A stack of newspapers towered to one side of a sagging corduroy sofa. Tall galoshes sat next to the door beneath a coat hanger holding only stained utility coveralls.

Again, her stomach lurched, and she glanced back to the stove, on top of which sizzled a cast-iron pan. Though she couldn't see from where she sat, she knew it was bacon.

She twisted again to see around the room. Finally, her eyes rested on a sign that hung next to the door. It was a metal rectangle whose corners were worn to faded nubs. Rust obscured some of the lettering, but it still read clear.

Hogtown
Founded by Bernard "Blackie" Zick

She was in Logan Zick's rotten, old cabin.

CHAPTER 46

"Hello?" Bo cried through the room.

It made no sense. It was a mistake. A game, maybe. A bad joke. How had she fallen asleep? What time was it?

Her phone. She looked down at her lap, searching her front pockets. She couldn't see it or feel it. She looked around at the floor for her satchel. She had to call someone.

But first, she had to free herself. Taking a deep breath, Bo thought hard. She thought about what she and Paul had been talking about. About where she was. Who might be here. Logan, for sure.

No clock glowed from the dark log walls. The only pop of color came from the white teeth of the various animal heads. No television set hummed behind her in the living room. No lights shone out from the short hallway that undoubtedly led to Logan's bedroom and bathroom.

The window next to the front door was covered with a tatty flannel curtain. It was growing dark out. Maybe it was just after sunset. Maybe she was crazy. The last thing

Bo remembered was bee-lining for Logan's cabin, ready to confront the old man about three dead kids. Had he taken her for a trespasser and wigged out? She cleared her throat and cried out again in hope. "Hello? Logan? Is anyone here?"

A pip from the back bedroom echoed back to her, but Bo couldn't tell if it was a reply or the squeak of a rotted floor board. She tried again. "Hello? Logan? Mr. Zick?"

She started to scoot herself backward to get a better view out the front window, but a leg of her chair caught on the lip of a floorboard and sent her crashing toward the door in time for the rev of a truck engine to drown her cries and the sound of her fall.

"Dang it," she seethed through clenched teeth. Her head throbbed and pain coursed through the length of her body, which now drooped from its bearings to the mucky wooden floor. "Help!"

She cried again, over and over, for some minutes before succumbing to her scorching lungs.

Another pip came from the back. "Mr. Zick?" Bo croaked.

No reply.

She jimmied her wrists against the chair back and wriggled her feet. Finding her bindings to be secure and impossible, she rolled to her chest and knees, grunting and thrusting as she did.

There was no way she could right herself. But the chair back was low, and she could easily scrape her way across the room.

She looked to the kitchen for any obvious knife block. But this being real life and not a movie, none appeared.

Instead, she chose to head in the direction of the pip. Clearly, if Logan was around, he didn't much care that she'd woken up. So Bo wasn't going to care if he found her. If there was one thing she knew, it was that she had to fight. Her brothers and father had always admonished the Delaney women: Delaneys don't negotiate. You put up a fight, or you die.

Bo wasn't about to die. She had too much to do.

She sucked in a breath, steadied herself against the floor with her forehead, and then fell to her side. From there, inch by inch, she scooted across the floor. Dust wads, errant hairs, and dirt collected along her thigh and abdomen as she moved from the kitchen to the living room and into the hallway. From there, it was clear there was just one bedroom and one bathroom.

"Hello!" Bo called out into the dark rooms. "Logan?"

The pip from before now came as a moan.

Bo thrust her hips forward down the hall, dragging her chair-laden body into the hallway. The wooden legs caught for a moment, but a quick adjustment freed her and she successfully wiggled into the doorway of the bathroom.

There, peeking over the lip of the bathtub, hogtied and duct-taped, was Brittany.

CHAPTER 47

Relief and dread swelled in Bo's chest. Though her mouth was not taped like Brittany's, Bo was speechless. Brittany began to cry, or at least, that's what Bo could make of her face, because half was covered in mud-caked duct tape and half was obscured by her matted blonde hair. She lifted her head as well as she could to peer over the ledge of the rust-spotted tub and locked eyes with Bo, who found her voice.

"Did Logan do this?"

Brittany nodded her head, tears falling onto the tape and streaking through the dirt.

"Brittany, it's going to be okay. I'll get us out of here. I promise. Have you seen Logan recently?" Bo craned her neck to search for the old man before looking back at Brittany, who was rocking herself up and flipping over onto her back. Tears welled in Bo's eyes as she took in the cramped bathroom. From her position on the floor, Bo could see a lidless, murky toilet. Yellow streaked from the lip down to the base of the pot.

The smell of bacon had long given way to urine and

feces, body odor, and filth. The bathroom, which at one point was likely charming and cozy, now did nothing more than house Logan's shit and piss. And, obviously, Brittany. Crushed beer cans and toilet paper rolls spilled out of the pedestal sink, which was missing a faucet anyway.

Brittany continued to wriggle into a new position from within the deep clawfoot tub. Bo thought hard. She could probably squirm her way to the front door, but there was no way she could open the door. Was there another way in or out? Were there scissors or knives available? She whispered all these questions to Brittany, who'd begun to sob in muffled chokes.

Bo jerked her hands and feet impotently until she heard tires crawl over gravel out front.

Keegan.

It had to be. He was on his way. He would know something happened. As soon as he couldn't find her. He'd know. She scooted on her hip back down the hallway, hissing to Brittany that they were safe. Her boyfriend was there. He'd save them. Her moans grew louder, but a feeling of dread welled in her stomach.

The front door began to open.

It wasn't Keegan.

It was Logan.

"Got dammit, Delaney. Get your ass back to the table. I done fried your bacon, and you're damn well gon' eat it."

Bo froze, swallowing through the oversized lump in her throat. Sweat broke out along the small of her back and the fine hairs along her flesh rose. Her stomach tightened and she braced herself as he drew near, tracking mud across his floor before he bent over to swing her up onto all four chair legs.

Then, in as quick a motion, he grabbed her chair back and dragged her to the table, twisting the chair back into her original position.

Then, without explanation, he untied her hands. "I don't mean to hurt you, woman." His voice wasn't soft, but gone was the poisonous undercurrent she'd seen the day the first body turned up.

If it weren't for the journalist in her, she'd have pushed up from the table and socked him hard before untying her legs and fleeing to the bathroom to grab Brittany.

But she had to know. She had to know the story. She had to *write* the story.

So instead of taking her opportunity to escape, Bo took a deep breath and accepted her plateful of bacon with a timid smile. "Thank you."

He grunted and returned to the skillet to dig out the remaining slices before sliding them onto a greasy rag and stalking back to the bathroom.

The sound of tape ripping away from skin preceded Brittany's scream. A dull thud killed the sound, and Logan returned to the kitchen empty-handed. Bo gripped the plate and faced forward, away from his heavy footsteps. She'd get her story all right. With or without him.

As soon as Bo smelled him, she twisted with all her weight and might, swinging the enamelware plate up and directly into the old man's face, where it cracked like a pistol against his nose. Blood and bacon grease filled the dank room, and Bo heaved herself down onto Logan, who'd fallen to his knees. She tackled him backward against the floor and pinned his wiry wrists with her shaking hands. Now untethered from the chair back, she had enough mobility to bring her knees up to his chest and apply all her weight.

Logan gasped for air, but he never once asked for mercy. Instead, his sunken, unseeing eyes stared beyond her.

Two could play that game. Bo cocked her fist back and drove her knuckles into Logan's scabby face once. Twice. Three times.

He wasn't dead.

But he was close enough.

She twisted around and worked at the knots on her ankles, freeing herself in moments before chucking the bloodied rope and dashing to the bathroom, where she untied Brittany and dragged her body from the tub. Bo checked her pulse, and after she found it, she hooked her hands under Brittany's arms and pulled her as fast as she could to the front door.

She went back in to see that Logan was still out. She glanced around the room for a phone. In seeing none, she looked instead for her satchel. Bo had to decide between wasting time finding it and making an attempt to escape with Brittany's half-dead weight.

There was a third option. On a whim, Bo raced to the kitchen drawers and recklessly yanked each one open. A mess of silverware clattered this way and that. Bo grabbed a knife. Just in case.

Keegan would arrive anytime, she just had to make it far enough away from Old Man Zick.

She tucked the knife into her back pocket and grabbed

Brittany again, dragging her over pine needles and lava rock and out to Hogtown Lane, where she squinted through the darkening sky to catch a hint of headlights. Someone. Anyone. Keegan.

She paused and glanced over her shoulder before continuing, but when she did, her blood froze.

Standing in his doorway was Logan. Shotgun steady in his grasp. Pointing directly at her.

CHAPTER 48

Keegan meandered back to his truck parked at the far side of the lake. When he had first arrived, the place was empty. Even Logan's truck wasn't sitting in his overgrown driveway. No police cruisers. No one working the lake. Most importantly, no Bo.

Surely, she wouldn't have tried to enter Logan's cabin. She had way more sense than that. Then again, she had seemed . . . eager. But he had told her to keep her distance. Walk the woods. So that was where he started. Walking into the woods and calling for her.

Once he gave up that effort, he grew nervous. The lake was a ways off from Maplewood Boulevard. If she'd started walking, he'd have seen her. But he hadn't. So she couldn't have walked.

Dread spread through him as he returned to his truck and pulled out his phone. Someone else had to know about this. Had to know her hunch. Had to know there might be an emergency. He shot a text to his friend Carl and pulled himself back into the cab.

But as he looked out his windshield toward the old cabin nearly sinking into the earth, the front door opened.

Logan Zick ambled out with a long-barreled gun hanging from his hand. Keegan squinted hard through the dusky evening sky. Was Logan about to kick him off the lake shore for trespassing?

No.

Instead, Logan drew the weapon and pointed it a hundred yards in the other direction. Toward the road.

Toward the most bizarre image Keegan ever could have conjured.

Bo Delaney and Brittany Cutler.

CHAPTER 49

Everything happened fast. The sound of the gunshot. Bo falling to the asphalt. Keegan screaming across the water and echoing between the pine trees.

Bo opened her eyes to see Brittany hovering over her face, her tears falling onto Bo, who wiped her face in time for Keegan to drop next to her and cup a hand under her head. "Bo, are you okay?"

Was she?

She took stock of her body and patted her chest and abdomen. Nothing. She felt fine. Keegan took her hand and pulled her to her feet before he drew a finger and pointed it in the direction of Logan, whose body lay crumpled on his front deck. Gunless. Lifeless.

———

The ensuing hours were a blur.

Paramedics released Bo from the ambulance. Her cuts

weren't severe, but a prescription of antibiotics would await her at the pharmacy. She'd get to it later.

Brittany had to be treated at Maplewood Regional, where only her parents visited her. The Delaney family considered Bo's act of heroism to be sufficient. They had nothing more to say to the wanton flatlander.

Police searched Logan's cabin to find nothing new, same as when they'd searched it right after the first body was found. At that time, his truck was also clear. Now, however, it was the scene of a crime. Four crimes, actually.

Brittany's testimony corroborated Bo's hunch, but that information didn't happen to include the fine details of the triple murder of the three college tourists. What they did learn was that Brittany had called Paul Zick, who was not the same person who came to pick up Brittany. When a gruff, older man arrived at Wood Smoke, he told her he was Paul's brother and ran a livery car and would take her to a motel for a small fee. She agreed. At one point in the car ride, she'd fallen asleep. During that time, they'd stopped in the woods, though she wasn't sure where. Logan returned to the truck in time to catch Brittany peek underneath the tarp in the back seat of his pick-up.

He didn't want to kill her, he said. He had enough blood on his hands, he said. But he couldn't let her go, either, he said.

So, they returned to his cabin, where he tied her up while handling the others.

That was as much as she knew. Between that ugly night and the evening Bo showed up at the cabin, Logan had tried to feed her fried fish and bacon. She refused it but did accept warm milk twice a day. In that time, Logan had complained to Brittany about tourists and Maplewood trash, accusing them of trespassing on his property and making a mockery of him. She'd put two and two together before he ever admitted to shooting the tourists on sight.

Brittany claimed that at one point, she was nearly positive Paul and his friend from the bar had arrived at Logan's cabin and nosed around outside. Despite her moans and thrashing in the tub, they never stepped foot beyond the front door, as far as she could tell. They never came in looking for her. They never tried to help her.

Logan eventually explained to Brittany that she hadn't done anything wrong except be curious, which confused him.

By the time Bo had shown up, Brittany fully expected to die in that bathtub. Her meager thanks came in the form of never again visiting the little mountain town.

Once the investigation wrapped up, Bo thought long and hard about picking up and leaving. Heading back to Tucson or trying out a new state. Maybe somewhere far away.

CHAPTER 50

They were in his bed, her finger drawing circles on his chest.

Bo breathed in and let out a long sigh. "I'm bad luck."

Keegan twisted to face her, tucking a strand of her dark hair behind her ear. He reached his face to hers and kissed her on the cheek before bouncing himself out of bed and over to his coffee maker. On his way, he called over his shoulder. "I disagree."

She pushed herself up and threw the covers aside before crossing to the table and sinking into a chair. "How? I come to Maplewood, one woman is kidnapped, and three are killed. A Maplewood legend, no matter how evil, is now dead. How am I not bad luck?"

"Those guests? The ones who ended up in the bottom of a hog farmer's lake? I'd say they're the ones who had bad luck. Not you. Not your family or mine. Not the Zicks, either. Not even Brittany. In fact, she might be the luckiest of us all."

She nodded in solemn agreement. They'd already

talked the whole thing to death and then talked some
more.

Keegan came to realize just how scummy his dad could
actually be. Even if Bob Flanagan was largely excluded
from any question of foul play, that he was such good
friends with Paul Zick was enough to push him to cancel
his run for re-election in the fall. Victoria threatened
divorce. Keegan cut contact for the time being.

Paul and Stewart were forced by the county prosecutor
to give up the paper for the duration of the trial. As it
hung in limbo, Paul had his lawyer ask Bo to stay on as
editor-in-chief while things could be figured out. He
claimed he trusted her. That she cared about the community. That he always intended to promote her.

She agreed to handle daily operations temporarily,
arguing that she was too green to be in charge and too
restless to make anything a career, even journalism.

Keegan had a good feeling that would change, especially when Bo asked to stay with him for the rest of the
summer. After all, Kurt was spending more time at the
lodge to be with Mary.

Bo admitted she wanted what her sisters all had.

And she wanted it with Keegan.

He wanted her, too.

———

In the days following Bo and Brittany's discovery, more
details unfolded. The police investigation was shared
publicly. Michael and Kara really were the prime suspects

for the duration of the case. Michael had already threatened a lawsuit. Kara convinced him to drop it.

Everyone had written off Logan as a grumpy hermit. No one thought he was belligerent enough to kill.

Evidence pointed to a pat story in which the three kids trespassed, which Logan took seriously. Had the lake actually been his property, Logan might have gotten away with a lesser sentence (if he'd survived Keegan's aim). The college trio was foolish to wander off the beaten path, but they were well within their rights.

Alas, the lake was public property.

Brittany's testimony only served to cast a light shade of suspicion on Paul, who would later be found innocent of any wrongdoing. That was the way in a small town. Those who lived on top of the mountain tended to stay there, even in the darkest of times.

And those who lived on the outskirts of town, no matter their connections, tended to stay there, too.

Logan Zick would be buried in the family plot down the road from Hogtown Lake.

His fishing cabin would continue to rot into the earth.

———

If you liked Bo Delaney, meet *Kit West* in *Silent Desert*.

Join the author's newsletter and stay up to date with new releases. Visit sebromke.com.

ACKNOWLEDGMENTS

Without the following people, *Silent Mountain* would be a wisp of smoke.

A big thanks to Jeff Robinson, Laura Bollin, Kaja Nelson, and Katie DeLav for reading the story in its infancy and providing valuable insight on the development of the characters and narrative flow.

My proofreader, Tamara Beard of Wrapped Up Writing: thank you for going above and beyond the call of duty. So glad to have connected with you. You really can make a book sing.

Mom and Dad, your investment in my career is crucial. Thank you!

Ed and Eddie, thank you for your encouragement and unending support on the home front.

ABOUT THE AUTHOR

S.E. Bromke is the author of *Silent Mountain*, her debut thriller. She writes contemporary women's fiction and romance under Elizabeth Bromke.

Bromke studied English and Spanish at the University of Arizona in Tucson where she graduated with honors. She now lives with her family in northern Arizona. In addition to writing books and teaching, she enjoys reading, watching movies, and spending time in the mountains.

Made in the USA
Coppell, TX
10 May 2021

55438118R00142